DIVORCE TOKEN

By Joyce Jenje -Makwenda

Joyce Jenje-Makwenda

This story was first published in Shona, with the title **GUPURO**, by JOYCE JENJE MAKWENDA - STORYTIME PROMOTIONS. It was translated into English by Sarudzayi Elizabeth Chifamba-Barnes. The fist edition was published by Lion Press 2009 .

The second edition is published by JOYCE JENJE MAKWENDA COLLECTION ARCHIVE (JJMCA) (STORYTIME PROMOTIONS) 2017.

A Joyce Jenje Makwenda Collection Archive Publication

Tel: +263 4 306336/ 306623
Cell: +263 773 468 378 / 775 220 026
info@joycejenjearchives.co.zw
joycejenje@gmail.com
www.joycejenjearchives.co,zw

ISBN   978-0-7974-8124-4

Divorce Token

A CIP record for this book is available from the British Library. It is also available at the Zimbabwe National Archives of Zimbabwe

Cover design: Ivor. W Hartmann, South Africa

ACKNOWLEDGEMENTS

The translation of Gupuro into English is a milestone in the literary history of Zimbabwe. While it is important to write in our African languages, it is also important to have these stories translated to other widely-used languages such as English. The translation of Gupuro (Divorce Token) into English would not have been possible were it not for the untiring spirit of Sarudzayi Chifamba-Barnes, who failed to enjoy her Christmas translating the book. Thank you for a great Christmas present my friend. Sarudzayi was also the first editor of the Shona version Gupuro. *Zvirambe zvakadaro Jeri wangu.* Thanks to Tinashe Mushakavanhu for editing this book, Sarudzayi Chifamba-Barnes and Ivor W. Hartmann for the cover and advice. I would also like to thank Jonathan Masere for his contribution. My friends and collegues thank you for the support and encuragement. Thanks to my family for always being there for me in many ways that I can not be able to mention because of space. I will always be grateful to my parents for naturing the artist in me, thank you Murehwa and MaDube; Always!

Thank you all for your support

Joyce Jenje Makwenda (2009)

DEDICATION

The novel is dedicated to all women who have had to go through oppression because of the traditional divorce token, "gupuro", and other forms of domestic violence. The book is a result of in-depth research undertaken by the author who gives an insight into the various ways through which women are abused by the use of a divorce token.

Prologue

"*Yowe! Yowe-e amaihwe!*" Netsai cried. She sat on the floor with a thud. If anyone had seen Netsai at that moment, one would have concluded that she was a mentally-ill intruder who had broken into someone's house. Her eyes were bulging as if she had just come face to face with a lion in a jungle with no room to escape. Her hair was untidy; the rollers that had been neatly put on earlier on looked like toy-spikes. Some rollers were still holding her hair firm, while others were now loose and hanging on thin strands of hair. She began to pull them from her hair; plucking them out, as if plucking feathers from a chicken.

"Where did Herbert put all that money? Whatever has entered into my house is certainly too big for my little boots." Netsai was muttering to herself as she put the clothes back into the wardrobe she had earlier thrown all over the room in search of the money. When she finished, she sat on the bed, with one hand supporting her chin. She was totally distressed.

Tsitsi knocked on the bedroom door, but Netsai didn't bother to respond. She called out to Netsai.

"Are you in, mama?" the maid asked. The question brought Netsai back from the world she was in.

"Is it you, Tsitsi?" Netsai responded with a question. "I was dosing," she said, wiping tears off her face.

"I brought the baby, I think she wants to breastfeed now," Tsitsi said, standing at the door.

"Come in, bring her," Netsai said.

Tsitsi got in the bedroom, and found Netsai squatting on the carpet. The room was a mess, with things tossed everywhere, as if someone had just moved in and hadn't had time to sort things out. Tsitsi passed the baby to Netsai. She didn't understand what was going on.

"Are you ok mama?" she asked, worried about her employer.

"I am alright. It's just a headache," Netsai responded. Tsitsi had already noticed that all was not well.

"Your headaches are becoming too much, mama. Why don't you go and see a doctor?"

Tsitsi was worried about Netsai's well-being and marriage. She knew something more than a mere headache was troubling Netsai.

"I took some pills. I will wait and see if they can help," Netsai replied, unbuttoning her blouse so that she could put Rutendo on the breast.

"Would you like me to prepare something to eat before I do the laundry?"

"Go ahead with your laundry. I will prepare the food myself when I am ready because I don't think I am going to work today. I feel as if one of my veins is going to burst anytime." Netsai's eyes were puffy and red, making it believable that she may be having a migraine, but they still did not disguise the fact that she had been crying as well.

"Go to a doctor, mama," Tsitsi repeatedly advised as she left the room, closing the door behind her.

She stood outside the room, leaning against the door for a little while, muttering, "Things change so fast. It's like a bad dream to think that this was one of the happiest families. Lord have mercy."

Tsitsi then went to empty the laundry basket in the bathtub where she did the laundry.

Tsitsi realized that they were out of laundry soap and went to remind Netsai. That month Netsai had not done her regular monthly shopping because she did not have enough money. Netsai advised Tsitsi to use another kind of soap; the *chimugondiya* blue bar to scrub the clothes with, and then boil some of the soap for soft clothes.

CHAPTER One

Kugarika tange nhamo woye-woye
Kugarika tange nhamo woye-woye
Sango rinopa waneta vasikana
Kugarika tange nhamo woye-woye!

It takes hard work to become rich,woye-woye
It takes hard work to become rich,woye-woye
And with hard work, the reward comes
It takes hard work to become rich,woye-woye!

Netsai was humming favourite song while sewing a dress. It was a traditional song that celebrates a person's accomplishment of desired goals. This was in the 1980s and the song was popular with the emerging class of the nation's cottage industry entrepreneurs. Netsai was wearing a Che Guevara beret, a t-shirt and, instead of a skirt, a wrapper was deftly and securely tied around her waist.

The only furniture in the sewing room was a small table, and a two-plate electric stove. The stove was placed on a roughly finished, homemade wooden shelf. The structure of the shelf made it obvious to any visitor that it was not bought in a commercial furniture store. The small working table was placed close to the main entrance into the room. This room served as the kitchen, the dining room and 'one-a cottage factory.'

When she finished sewing, Netsai removed the sewing machine from the table because she wanted to use the same table for ironing the dresses. The table had a multi-purpose function. It was a working table, an ironing board and a dining table, three in one. Netsai ironed the newly-finished dresses.

Adjacent to the room was another room where Netsai kept her newly made garments. The new garments were all neatly piled one on top of another.

As Netsai was putting the finished clothes away, she heard a knock on the door. She went to open the door to welcome the visitor, and found Rudo her neighbour's daughter.

"Oh, it's you Rudo!"

"Yes it's me. Good afternoon, aunty."

As they talked, the young visitor was leaning against the door, a sign that she did not want to get inside the house, or stay longer than was necessary. Although they were not related, Rudo called Netsai 'aunty' as a sign of respect. Calling an older person by their first name is considered disrespectful in the Shona culture. Any woman who is your mother's age is your 'aunt', and any woman your grandmother's age is your 'grandmother', or *gogo*. Likewise, any man old enough to be your father is your uncle, and any man old enough to be your grandfather is grandfather or *sekuru*. Such is the Shona custom in which honorific titles are very important.

"How was your day, Rudo?"

"I had a good day, aunty. You had a good day as well? *Mukoma* Luke sent me to ask if you are still going to town because he also wants to take someone to the hospital," Rudo said.

"Tell him to go without me. I am still working on my last dress. That's what delaying me."

"Ok, aunty I will tell him.

"He can come at 12 noon today. I will be ready. Why didn't you go to school today?" Netsai asked.

"We finished writing our exams and we are on vacation."

"Oh! By the way, you were doing GCSE Ordinary levels? I had forgotten," Netsai was amazed at how time had gone fast and how Rudo had grown.

"Yes, aunty. I am going home now," Rudo said as she turned and began walking towards her home.

"It's alright, Rudo. Do not forget. Twelve noon exactly! Do you hear me?" Netsai was shouting, as the little girl happily skipped towards her home, a distance away. She continued her work, rearranging and packing the finished garments into cardboard boxes.

When she finished packing the boxes, she started preparing lunch for her children, Farai and Tariro. She decided to leave the keys for her house with one of her tenants, *Mai*Chido. *Mai*Chido would give Farai and Chido the keys if they came back from school before she returned. She called out for *Mai*Chido, but there was no answer. *Mai*Chido was busy cajoling with her friends behind the house. After getting no response, Netsai eventually decided to take the keys to *Mai*Chido's room, where she found *Mai*Chido chatting and laughing with her friends. They were laughing as if nothing else mattered in the world.

"Umm, is everything alright with you today *madzimai*, for you to talk and laugh like you are going to spit your lungs out like that?" Netsai asked in jest.

"Ah, you are home? When I came I saw your door closed and assumed you were not around." *Mai*Jessica, one of the women said.

"Did you knock on my door and get no response....?" Netsai asked, but before she could get a response *Mai*Chido burst with laughter at one of the women's jokes. Tears of laughter were rolling down her chubby cheeks.

"These women want to kill me with laughter. Why do they make me to laugh like this?"

"Honestly?, I am saying the truth," *Mai*Frances said clasping her hands, shaking her head and gasping for breath all at once. "I did not greet you, *Mai*Farai, since you found us busy talking," she said, turning her head towards Netsai. The women addressed each other using the names of their first children. Netsai's first child was Farai so she was known as *Mai*Farai.

"Umm, it's your time, *vasikana*. Ladies. Let me leave you to it. Enjoy yourselves. Here are the house keys, *Mai*Chido. I am running late. Please, can you give them to Farai when he comes from school?" Netsai said, handing the keys to *Mai*Chido. Luke arrived at

Netsai's home at that very moment and blew the horn of his car. *Mai*Chido took the keys and Netsai left. As soon as she was gone, Netsai became the subject. "How do you live with this woman? A person who does not have time for other women?" *Mai*James asked. *Mai*James was known for bad mouthing other people. She had been given the nickname Radio Sixteen because of her penchant for gossip.

"There you go again," *Mai*Frances said disapprovingly as she tried to dissuade her friend from maligning other people.

"*Mai*Farai is a busy woman and hardly finds time to gossip. She does not like to waste time talking all day," *Mai*Chido said in an attempt to defend Netsai.

"*Mai*Chido, you talk as if you have any other choice. We all know that you don't have much of a choice here, but to defend *Mai*Farai. She is your landlady after all. You are afraid that she can terminate your tenancy and chuck you out of her house," *Mai*Jessica answered. She continued, "Where would you go, if she evicted you? Your life is in *Mai*Farai's hands!

"There are whispers that she is really a bad woman, that she uses *muti* to make money. Honestly, at her age, where did she get the money to achieve all these things, which older women like us have failed to achieve? Look at my hair, its turning grey, and I still haven't acquired as much as *Mai*Farai has. Apart from the miserable two-roomed cottage, I have nothing much?"

"You and your motor-running mouth!" *Mai*Frances said pointing a finger at *Mai*Jessica accusingly, trying to make her friend keep quiet.

"You think I don't know that her father uses witchcraft and sorcery to amass other people's wealth? This woman is a benefactor of her father's wicked witchcraft."

The other two women laughed dismissively at what *Mai*James was insinuating. She continued her rant.

11

"A -ah, don't you see how short and dark she is? She has the witch's look! *Munhu wepi anobva ashaya nechimiro chese*, what kind of woman is she that she is even structure-less?"

"What can she do about her body structure and complexion as these are God-given features that can not be easily changed? Her weight looks proportional to her body and structure and she chooses good clothes that go with her slim built," *Amai*Frances disagreed with *Mai*James. "Why do you always think people with light complexion are beautiful and those with a dark complexion are ugly? Is that not being a bit shallow?"

"Beauty! I don't know why that husband of hers is wasting his time and handsome face with her? What a mis-match?" *Mai*James said.

"Let's not talk about that, please!" *Mai*Chido, was getting uncomfortable with *Mai*James' slanderous remarks.

"You work hard and where does all your money go to? This woman, through her witchcraft powers takes it, and you sit there blindly not realising what is happening to you! That woman is evil. She does not have time to greet or chat with anyone. What a woman....?"

*Mai*Frances stopped *Mai*James in mid sentence.

"What is wrong with you? Whenever there is a successful farmer, the farmer will always have lazy people as neighbours. I can't listen to this any longer, let me go back to my house, *Mai*Chido," she said; standing up, ready to leave.

*Mai*Jessica, who had been responding with gestures and laughter also left at the same time. *Mai*Chido was relieved because the discussion had suddenly turned into a campaign against her landlady's industriousness.

* * *

Divorce Token

When Netsai was dropped off by *Mukoma* Luke, she went to one of the shop owners she supplied with the clothes she made. After showing the buyer the things she had sewn, they began to negotiate payment. After inspecting all the garments, the buyer looked satisfied. He signed a cheque of Z$10 000 and gave it to her. Netsai was so excited that she literally ran to the bank to deposit the cheque in a bank account she jointly owned with her husband. It was as if she thought the buyer might change his mind.

* * *

Herbert was enjoying his lunch break and chatting to work colleagues. He had joined a queue to buy sadza, a thick porridge made from maize meal. Herbert's colleague, Peter, was a calculating miser who had the habit of bringing small amounts of money not sufficient enough to buy a meal, and asking Herbert or any of his workmates to top up his payment. On this day Herbert, who was now fed up with Peter's habit, refused to make up the deficit, telling Peter that he had only brought enough money to buy himself a meal. Peter on realizing that Herbert was not going to help him out, decided to threaten and embarrass Herbert with the negative rumours that were making the rounds about him.

"You know what I would do if I was you Herbert? I would share the money that you are getting from dirty deals with me your true friend so that tomorrow when you are in prison I bring you food. Don't be mean," Peter said, trying to blackmail Herbert into giving him money.

"If its money from dirty deals, then why do you want it?"

"Mr Kudzingwa," interrupted the canteen worker, "Did you order *sadza* and chicken? Here it is!" The canteen lady passed the plate of *sadza* and roasted chicken to Herbert.

"Next please!" The lady said, signaling to Peter that she was ready to take his order. "What shall I serve you?"

Peter was still deciding on what to pick, not that he had much choice, considering the amount of money he had.

Herbert looked at his colleague, did not offer to pay for his lunch and took his sadza to sit at a table in the eating area of the canteen. Another colleague joined Herbert at his table.

Peter, who usually shared a table with Herbert most of the times, walked past Herbert's table and went to sit at a different table with other men.   He was disappointed that his friend had refused to buy him a better meal, now he had to do with *sadza* and veggie, like a prisoner.

Peter's remarks were getting crude and personal targeting Herbert, "A caterpillar in cow-dung also thinks it's a cow as well," Peter hissed through his teeth.   "When a poor man sits with the rich he thinks that he is rich as well!"

The other men couldn't make head or tail of what Peter was talking about. They didn't comment. Herbert was in a deep conversation at his table, not minding his ranting friend.

"Herbert tell us about your deals, everyone keeps talking about, how you are making a lot of money? Please share your money-making recipe with us, please Herbert?" the man sharing the table with Herbert pleaded.

"Deals? I don't do any illegal deals. Don't take my friend Peter seriously. I get my money from selling the clothes that my wife sews, you know my wife has a sewing business.....," Herbert was abruptly interrupted by another colleague who wanted to know when Herbert was going to deliver a dress he had ordered from his wife. The talk about Herbert's deals was soon forgotten as Herbert entertained this client.

"If you forget to bring orders to your customers, how will you get the money? Don't forget your pot-belly is full of our monies! " Mr Chuma said as he ribbed Herbert in a collegial gesture.

Herbert laughed.

Most of Herbert's work mates ordered clothes from his wife. Every month-end, when people got paid, Herbert usually went home with a thick ward of notes, money collected from workmates who would have ordered clothes for their families. Netsai was popular at Herbert's work place. It was as if she worked there, too. When Herbert was leaving work that day, the security guard at the main gate stopped him. He ordered Herbert out of the car, something which he had never done before. The security guard searched the car inside out. Herbert was speechless. The guard had never searched him so thoroughly before. Herbert was also body searched. The security guard had always been friendly to Herbert. They had always conversed whenever he was passing through the gate. That day things had changed.

After searching him, the guard ordered Herbert to move. Herbert remained standing near his car for a little while, confused. The guard was angrily barking at him.

"Go! Go! You are holding up traffic. Don't you see the queue behind you?" The guard waved Herbert away.

"What is wrong today, *mudhara?*" Herbert asked.

"Next!" the guard barked without bothering to answer the baffled Herbert. Dumbfounded, Herbert got into his car and drove away. The sequence of events that day began to unfold the more he thought about what had transpired. He tried to figure out Peter's resentment and anger. Peter knew that Netsai was a hard-working woman and he resented Herbert because of that. His envy made him to try to influence others to believe that Herbert was involved in underhand deals.

The security guard's action seemed to reinforce Peter's callow remarks. Herbert shook his head and said to himself, "It looks like I am being persecuted because of my wife's hard work!"

When Netsai had finished her business in the city, she bought goodies for her children and went home laden with their favourite toys and food, including chicken and chips, her children's favourite meal.

When Tariro saw her mother, she ran to embrace her, singing "*Mauya mama*, (welcome mum!). Tariro took the parcels from her mother and carried them into the house, where Netsai found her son Farai drying the dishes that he had just finished washing.

Tariro was younger than Farai. She was in Grade Five and a clever girl too.

"Welcome home, *mama* (mum)," Farai said.

Like his sister, he was happy to see his mother. He embraced her, smiling and revealing big white teeth.

"Do you ever give yourself any time to rest, Farai?" Netsai asked her hardworking son. " You are already cleaning the dishes?"

"I rested after I came from school. I bought the meat for our supper and have already cooked it," Farai said.

"Thank you my beloved son," Netsai was pleased with her son.

Farai was a very well disciplined boy who loved his mother dearly and tried to help her with house chores whenever he could. He was also very intelligent and came top in class for all his end of year exams. He was still in primary school, Grade Seven.

After settling down, and her children having opened their parcels, Netsai asked her daughter, Tariro to take a portion of the chips to *Mai*Chido. When she came back, she sat down with her brother and they ate the other portion. They were a happy family and anyone who saw them could clearly see their happiness.

Later when Netsai and Herbert were having their supper of beef stew and *sadza*, it became obvious to Netsai that Herbert had something troubling his mind. He was not his usual self and seemed worried. He was wondering whether to tell his wife about what had happened at work; the accusations of performing illegal deals and the harassment from the security guard, but decided against it. He did not want to worry his wife. Netsai put Herbert's unusual behaviour to tiredness. She decided to cheer him up by giving him a bottle of his favourite ice-chilled beer. That did the trick because Herbert began to be more relaxed and jovial with every sip of the beer.

"Thank you, Netsai my darling. You just know the right tonic to cure my tired body. Now I can sleep well," Herbert said, pouring beer into a glass.

"I could see that you were really tired," said Netsai, relieved that her husband was now in a colourful mood again.

"Where are the children, Tariro and Farai? Why are they not eating *sadza* with us?" Herbert asked.

"I don't think they have enough room in their stomachs for any *sadza* tonight. They just ate fresh chips which I bought for them in town," Netsai replied.

"Oh, I see. Are you loaded today?" he asked

"You forget I delivered that big order to that Indian shop owner in town?"

"Oh, I had forgotten about that! So, where are my chips? " Herbert asked in a soft tone; mischief veiled in romantic subtlety.

"Are you talking about real chips, or you want something else?" Netsai asked. She had noticed the naughty twinkle in her husband's eyes. "Do you mean those other chips?"

They both laughed. Netsai took her wallet out of her handbag. She pulled out a ward of dollar notes and handed them to her husband, saying, "Next time you should buy proper lunch at work instead of keeping money in your pocket while you starve yourself."

"You know that this money you give me to buy lunch is buying me hatred from other workmates instead?" Herbert then told Netsai about what had happened at work that day. As they were discussing Herbet's concerns, Tariro came into the room, asking for assistance with her homework. Farai was behind her.

"Dad, can you help me with this Maths problem?" Tariro asked her father, showing him her book.

"I am not really good in solving Maths problems. You better ask your mother who, as a businesswoman, spends most of her time calculating figures," Herbert said, handing the book to Netsai.

"Dad, are you saying mum is cleverer than you?" Tariro innocuously laughed at her father.

"I am good at other things, Tariro. Remember I helped you with your Shona and History assignments and you got the best marks in class, right?" Herbert said.

"Yes dad, I remember that proverb you taught me, the one that says *imbwa nyoro ndidzo tsengu dzematore*, dogs that look humble and harmless are the ones that chew and swallow tougher things like cowhides. You know what another boy in my class said about that, when the teacher asked him to explain the meaning of the proverb?"

"What did he say?"

"He said a dog is only humble just after it has had a shower!" Everyone laughed.

Netsai helped Tariro with her Maths homework, and soon after, the children returned to their study room.

Herbert and Netsai took out more drinks from the fridge and drank while watching television. Netsai took their joint account bank book and showed her husband the deposit she had made that day. There was Z$35 000 balance in the account.

Herbert could not believe his eyes when he saw the new balance.

"We have a lot of money now. I was thinking it was still Z$20 000!"

"You know what Herbert? I think we should buy building material and finish extending this house."

"Maybe, but I was talking to an Estate Agent today and he told me that with the money we already have in our savings, the Z$20 000 that I still thought to be the balance, we could buy a bigger and better house in the low density suburbs," Herbert said.

"You can't be serious!" Netsai looked at Herbert straight in the eyes in utter disbelief. "You must be joking," she said.

"You think people who live in those low density suburbs have plenty of money? It's all bank loans and nothing more. If you know how to handle debts, then you can live large in the posh suburbs."

"I am not keen on borrowing money and accruing debts, *Baba*vaFarai." Netsai liked to call her husband *Baba*vaFarai when discussing serious family matters.

"If we rent this house out, it will earn us enough money to pay off the mortgage that we will be paying for the low density suburb home." Herbert said, much to Netsai's excitement.

"If you want to find out more about buying a house in the suburbs, we can go and find out from my friend who works for an Estate Agent. He can give us a better insight and explanation."

"Herbert, don't forget that it is only people with cars who can afford to live in those areas. You want us to humiliate ourselves by asking for lifts from other residents?"

"Those are big areas and no one will pry into your private life," Herbert was trying to convince Netsai that they could fit in the low-density suburbs too. "Besides, I use the company car more often. We can buy ours later on."

After a few drinks, Herbert and Netsai went out to admire the work they had done on the house. They had built the house from the first brick into a fine eight-roomed house. They inspected the water tape, which needed to be repaired. Even though their house had eight rooms, they only used four rooms, and rented the other four to lodgers. They had just finished plastering the inside, and were now left with plastering the outside.

Netsai was worried about abandoning the plastering project and embarking on something new and spending more money than they could afford. Herbert was less concerned about that because his heart and mind was now set on a bigger house in a better suburb. He was aching to go and live in one of those expensive, big houses with big yards, in the quiet and spacious low-density areas.

CHAPTER Two

Netsai hardly slept that night. Her mind was preoccupied with the idea of meeting the Estate Agent, after her husband had convinced her that they needed to move on. Even though she bought the idea, she had reservations about consulting estate agents. This was something she had never done before. Their current house in Glen View high-density suburbs had been bought through a housing cooperative scheme, which her husband had joined at work. Under this housing scheme, employees contributed towards the purchase of stands and once they finished paying the monthly instalments, they were allowed to build their houses at their own pace.

Netsai woke up at dawn to carry out basic house chores and prepare her children for school. As soon as Tariro and Farai had left for school, Netsai and Herbert went to see the estate agent in town. The estate agent was a gregarious man who made his potential clients as comfortable as possible.

"So you have now decided to move to areas where the rich live?" *Va*Gwaku asked as he joyously welcomed them into his office. It was more of a remark than a question. "You have decided to leave the noises of the ghetto, *Mai*Farai. In the leafy suburbs where you want to move to, the only noise you will hear will be the singing birds and barking dogs," Mr Gwaku said while pulling out a document with the latest houses on the market.

"We have decided to follow you to the low-density suburbs," Herbert broke the silence that had filled the room.

*Va*Gwaku began to advertise the houses on the market, a trade he was very good at. He showed the couple a list of the houses on the market, ranging between twenty thousand to thirty-five thousand dollars

"It's all up to you. These are some of the houses on offer. It's the size and depth of your pocket that counts. Let me know what you think," he said.

*Va*Gwaku told Herbert and Netsai that they could also apply for a loan or mortgage for the house. They could pay the mortgage over a period of twenty-five years, he explained.

Netsai and her husband exchanged glances, and Herbert said, "We don't need a mortgage or loan for the house."

*Va*Gwaku looked surprised.

"We want to pay cash," Herbert explained.

"*Babamudiki* don't tell me you have all this money. I don't think you can save enough money from the paltry wage you get for your job as a driver. It is such a prohibitively huge amount. Even most of these rich businessmen you see in town buy these houses on mortgage. Are you participating in these illegal dealings?" *Va*Gwaku looked shocked.

"No, *Va*Gwaku. I owe it to my ancestors and to God who blessed me with a very hard working wife. She is talented when it comes to sewing," Herbert replied. "She is also a very good small scale farmer, and that is why we have managed to raise all this money."

"Then you are very lucky indeed. We always fool ourselves into believing that only people in paid employment are the only ones capable of earning and saving money. How very wrong? Now, let me educate you about house buying in Harare. You do not pay the full amount when you buy a house. With the money you have, you can buy two houses at the same time and remain with enough change to even buy a car," *Va*Gwaku advised them.

"Ha, don't tell us that, *Mukoma*? How is that possible?" Herbert asked, looking at Netsai with excitement.

"Yes, it's possible. This is how you do it. You pay a deposit of ten thousand dollars for each house, and rent-out one house to a tenant. You can pay mortgage for that house with the money the tenants pay for rental. The mortgage for the house you are occupying will be paid by yourselves. The second house will be for *investment, Babamudiki.* This is how people live in town. You buy a car and put the rest of the money in the bank. Clever people make hay while the sun is still shining."

*Va*Gwaku was a skilled salesman. When he talked about business, he spoke with panache and an infectious enthusiasm like that of a preacher. Herbert and Netsai nodded their heads in unison, smiling at what *Va*Gwaku had just said.

"*Mukoma*, when a man has a full belly, he does not say goodbye. Give us the rest of today to discuss the option you have given us. We will come back to you tomorrow," Herbert spoke, as he and his wife stood up and left the office.

"In fact if you have time tomorrow, we can drive around to view three houses which I haven't advertised yet," *Va*Gwaku suggested.

"You talk about time? We have all the time in the world. I will not go to work tomorrow," Herbert said, as a matter of fact. The three of them laughed.

"I will come to pick you up at your house tomorrow at eight in the morning," *Va*Gwaku said.

"Thank you *Va*Gwaku. *Kutenda kwekitsi kuri mumoyo*, a cat will never say thank you, but it will still be grateful in its heart," Netsai was thanking *Va*Gwaku. She emphasized her gratitude by clapping her hands.

"I am the one more grateful, because you are bringing business into the company," Mr Gwaku said.

"See you tomorrow *Mukoma*," Herbert said.

On their way home, the couple was thrilled by the prospect of owning two houses in a low density suburb. They were still not convinced that it was possible. *VaGwaku* was a credible man who had a good reputation and had assisted a lot of people to acquire properties. He was well known for his unfettered help to his clients. He had helped people from all walks of life.

Netsai and Herbert were too excited to talk.

"You know Herbert; it is very difficult to find a genuine and honest agent like *VaGwaku*. These are the kind of people who go to heaven when they die. There are plenty of dishonest people around." They both laughed genially.

"You remind me of our friend VaKuneta and his family. They are going to be shocked when they find out that we are moving to the suburbs.

"You talk as if we have already bought the house. It is not wise to count the number of chicks you have before the eggs are hatched," Netsai reminded her husband.

"Whatever, it's better to try than never. Sometimes you must just dream on, you never know where that dream will take you," Herbert said. In his mind, he was already in the *suburbs*.

As the couple went back home, they looked happy and giddy. If things worked out, they would be proud owners of three houses. This was a dream come true, a rags to riches transformation.

The following morning *VaGwaku* went to pick up Herbert and Netsai in his car so as to show them the three houses on the market. Netsai and Herbert were overwhelmed.

Noticing their anxiety, *VaGwaku* assured his clients that there was nothing to be afraid of. He gave them time to view the houses, to get inside and walk around the gardens. At one of the houses, the couple found the white owners still there, who willingly showed them around the house explaining all the rooms and their purposes. Herbert and Netsai could still not believe that they could own such property. The owners explained that they were selling their house because they were returning to the United Kingdom.

They visited and viewed a house in Eastlea suburb, which impressed them. They just nodded their heads, awe-struck and lost for words to describe the beauty of the house.

"Why are you quiet as if you have been attacked by zombies or ghosts?" *VaGwaku* teased, jokingly. He knew the house had registered a deep positive impression with the young couple.

"*Mukoma*, this is an amazing property. Do you think we can leave our high density house to come and occupy one of these immaculate houses?" Herbert said, shaking his head.

"Herbert, it's very possible. If you do not buy these houses now, you might never be able to buy them. House prices are going up with each passing year. Last year, 1983, houses were much cheaper than they are now. Now the houses are becoming more and more expensive," *VaGwaku* advised.

"Ah, *Mukoma*!" Herbert sighed. He was at a loss for words.

"This is the time, Herbert. Don't let other people mislead you by creating an impression that buying a house in the *suburbs* is an impossible thing to do. If this is the house that you want, I can organize it for you now, and come month-end you will become the new proud owners." *VaGwaku* said, pointing at the house.

"I really like it, but I am worried about the mortgage rates for such a beautiful house." Netsai said. She had fallen in love with the house. Her husband was too excited to say anything.

"That information and terms of the mortgage will come from the bank. But as I said, you have enough money to get two houses, and leaving you with excess to pay your premiums. You must believe me. I was born in the city."

VaGwaku was born in the sprawling black township of Mbare. To be born and bred in such areas meant one became a natural skilled survivor and negotiator, always outmanoeuvring competitors. The townships were like jungles, only the fittest survived.

"*Mukoma*," said Herbert, "you have to educate me because, as you know, I am an SRB (Strong Rural Background)." They all laughed. "I am serious, *Mukoma*, I have a very strong rural background and I am not well versed with these urban tricks."

"Don't worry, I will sort out everything for you," *va*Gwaku said, opening the car door for Netsai and Herbert. They were going to see and view another house.

They settled for the house in Estlea and another in Milton Park. They did not want to procrastinate, and went to a Building Society straight away, where they were told what to do. They promised to return to the Building Society the next day.

The following morning, *Va*Gwaku found Netsai and Herbert waiting for him outside his office. They did not waste time. Their minds were made up. Without wasting time, they began filling some forms. *Va*Gwaku handed them two forms, one to Herbert and another to Netsai, since they were buying two houses.

"One can fill in this one, while the other can fill in and sign the other form," *Va*Gwaku advised as he handed out the forms.

"My husband can sign both forms," Netsai pushed the form to Herbert.

"Why can't you?" *Va*Gwaku asked, giving Netsai a meaningful look. "You can put one house in your name while your husband can sign his name on another one," he expertly suggested, trying to appeal to Netsai to do the right thing.

"I don't see what difference it makes. What belongs to my husband also belongs to me," Netsai replied.

"If you don't want to sign the forms, I will sign both of them," Herbert told his wife.

*Va*Gwaku looked apprehensively at both Netsai and her husband, but controlled his emotions because he did not want to cause tension between the young couple.

He assisted Herbert in filling the forms. When he finished signing the forms, Herbert handed them to *Va*Gwaku. Herbert had not bothered to pass the forms to his wife for her to see what he had signed for; *Va*Gwaku noted with concern and passed the forms to Netsai to go through them and approve everything put down by her husband. Netsai was not interested. She glanced at them, paying scant attention and handed them back to *Va*Gwaku.

"I don't think *Babava*Farai could have made a mistake," Netsai told *Va*Gwaku.

"I just wanted to make sure you will not blame anyone tomorrow, saying you were not given the chance to check them," *Va*Gwaku replied, accepting the forms back from Netsai. He handed more forms to Herbert to sign and Netsai excused herself, leaving the two men to finalise the buys.

At the reception she began to chat with *Va*Gwaku's secretary, who asked Netsai about the two houses they were buying.

"Congratulations, *Amai*, for investing in houses," *Va*Gwaku's secretary congratulated Netsai. "How did you do it, I mean buying two houses at the same time? Have you finished signing the forms? Why did you leave *Va*Gwaku's office so early?" she asked.

"My husband is signing the forms," Netsai responded.

"You mean you are not putting the houses in joint ownership?" The secretary looked at Netsai disapprovingly.

"Does it matter if it's just my husband's name which appears on the title deeds? We all know that men head the families, and as such, are responsible for buying houses. Even if I don't sign, these houses belong to both of us," Netsai explained.

"You might regret this one day. You can't just put everything in your husband's name, when you have been working as hard for this moment," the secretary cautioned. She knew about Netsai's industriousness and felt the need to warn Netsai of the possible dangers that might result from her decision; not to have her name on the title deeds for the houses.

Netsai was annoyed by the secretary's remarks, and did not hide her anger. "When my husband is finished, will you be kind enough to tell him that I have gone out to buy a soft drink?" Netsai said, as she walked out of the office, away from the prying secretary.

"I will tell him," the secretary said, noticing that Netsai was annoyed with her questions.

Some women are jealous. I don't think this girl understands marriages and how they work. Umm! She looks like the type that is not married but yearns for a husband. Now she wants to spoil my marriage! Netsai thought, and hissed through her teeth.

When Herbert finished signing the forms, he paid *Va*Gwaku the deposit for both houses and thanked him for his assistance. But even as he shook hands with *Va*Gwaku, he still could not believe that he now owned two suburban houses.

"*Va*Gwaku, thank you very much. He who gives you a wild orange to eat is your kinsman," he said, clapping his hands.

"*Babamudiki*, they say you can only ask for directions from one who already has walked the path. I might be a short man, but my eyes have seen a lot," *Va*Gwaku intimated.

"*Vakuru vakati dzisiri nyimo makunguwo aidyei?* Our elders have a saying that it's because of groundnuts that crows are alive. What would they eat if it were not for groundnuts? Please, keep safe and stay away from the fire, you keeper of orphans," Herbert eulogized.

"That's my job *Babamudiki*," *Va*Gwaku said, walking Herbert out of his office.

That day Herbert and his family were over the moon. That night they did not sleep, celebrating their new houses, playing loud music, to the curiosity of neighbours who were oblivious of the new development.

Herbert and Netsai danced to songs that they used to dance to when they were still courting. Their minds wandered to the old golden days. They played Dolly Parton's, *Take My Hand;*, one of their wedding songs. Tired of dancing, they sat down, looked at their wedding photo album, kissed and hugged. They played their entire music collection, whilst drinking beer and soft drinks all night.

Farai and Tariro, who were peeping through the door, could not help notice their parents' excitement. Before too long, they were called to join in the celebrations. Tonight was different. Their mother was not sitting at her machine like she did everyday after supper, and their father was not busy reading his correspondence notes. Something big must have happened.

Tariro and Farai went to bed early, leaving their parents in the sitting room, and before they realized it, Netsai and Herbert were surprised to wake up cuddled on the floor. They had slept on the carpet in the sitting room. That night had felt like a honeymoon for them. Herbert looked shocked. He thought that their children could have seen them making love.

"Netsai, do you realize where we are?" Herbert asked nudging her in the ribs as he pulled a bed-sheet over his naked body.

"Don't worry, I locked the door. The kids saw nothing," Netsai said, and they both laughed. "You know Herbert, last night reminded me of the days when we were still boyfriend and girlfriend."

"We are supposed to do this all the time, Netsai, but because of other commitments and pressures, it's really difficult."

"We should not get carried away by the idea of a new house. What if something happens and we don't go to live there?"

"We already have the keys for the new house, remember, so what can possibly happen? You know what I want? A new baby to bless the new house! What do you think?"

The thought of another baby made Netsai's heart skip a beat. "Where will a new baby come from?"

"I think you forgot to take your contraceptive pills last night," Herbert said, showing Netsai the pills.

"Oh! My God! What?" Netsai registered shock as she realized what happened the night before.

"It's time for a third baby Netsai," Herbert assured her, but Netsai was too shocked to answer.

Soon, Farai and Tariro were counting down the number of days left before their family moved to Eastlea. Their parents had decided to rent out the Milton Park house. The idea of moving to a new school in a new place made the kids excited and spurred them to work hard. Their parents had made it clear that if they got poor grades, they would have to commute to their old school every day. And the children did not want that. They worked harder at school than ever before.

When the school session ended for the holidays, Netsai and Herbert finally moved to their new house in Eastlea. On the big day, friends and neighbours came to help them with the packing. Everyone was sad that they were leaving. Netsai was also sad to leave her friends and neighbours behind, but she had to move on and start a new life. As their hired van left their old house, Netsai and her children cried.

CHAPTER Three

Not everyone was pleased with Netsai and her family's departure. *Mai*James had not bothered to come to see them off. She witnessed the departure through her bedroom window.

"What does it help, to go and live in a posh area where they don't really belong? They will fill their refrigerators with sour milk and water!" she said to herself, as jealous nearly choked her, creating a huge lump in her throat. She contorted her face in disgust.

"They are now moving to an area where 'real' rich people live, not the 'fake' rich like them, good for these high density areas," she said, clasping her palms together. She felt like a lump of dry mud was stuck in her throat.

That night when Herbert returned from work, he found Netsai had already finished unpacking in their new home.

"Oh, you have already finished unpacking, Netsai?" Herbert said, admiring the living room where Netsai was.

"*Mai*Chido came along and helped me unpack. We finished unpacking in no time at all."

"Even then, it would not have taken longer to unpack our little, pathetic furniture. The living room looks as cavernous as a stadium because of its emptiness.

"Tariro and Farai," Netsai called her children, "you might as well turn the sitting room into a football pitch and play until you get tired." They all laughed.

"The most important thing is to have the house, furniture is something we can always acquire later," Netsai said.

The house was too big, and one could hear voice echoes bouncing off the myriad walls on the corridors even when they whispered. The curtains from their old house were too small to cover the big windows. Netsai did not have enough curtains and some of the windows were without curtains. They covered some of the windows with newspapers. Initially they had planned to move house mid year after buying new furniture and curtains, but decided to move in anyway. They didn't want to disrupt their children during the middle of a school term. They had instead used most of their savings to transfer their children to a school in Eastlea.

Netsai worked hard in the next few months to raise enough money to buy the new furniture they needed. Her sewing enterprise was thriving. She now rented a shop in the city centre, where she employed assistants to help her. She was also a cross-border trader, going to South Africa with handmade crafts She used the profit to buy electronic goods like radios and televisions because they had a market in Zimbabwe.

The other two houses were also generating money for the couple. They were receiving rentals from both houses. After four months of living in an empty house with windows covered with newspapers, Netsai and Herbert finally had the state-of-the-art furniture for their new big house; a very beautiful lounge suite, a hardwood mahogany dining room suite, a big four-plate cooker, a fridge and a freezer, carpets and curtains. The bedrooms were neatly furnished and looked like five-star hotel rooms. The cooker was so magnificent that one felt intimidated to cook anything on it, for fear of spoiling the food. It was a dream come true for the couple. They had also bought beautiful and comfortable garden chairs.

The house was big and had many rooms. It was like a maze.

In the early 80s, Herbert and Netsai appeared too young to own such a big property, and anyone seeing Herbert, wearing boxer-shorts and working in the garden could easily have mistaken him for a garden boy or a housekeeper. Netsai, who was slim and short, could easily have passed for a house maid. A visitor would only be convinced that the two were indeed the homeowners only after seeing their family photos displayed in the living room.

When Herbert's mother, *Va*Soda, came to visit them and to see the new house she had heard so much about, she refused to sit on the leather sofas. The old woman was not convinced that her son and his wife owned such immaculate property. She didn't want the 'real owner' of this *palace* to chase her away or accuse her of trespassing. She remembered the colonial days when blacks were required to apply for passes to be able to go to 'whites only' areas. Anyone without the pass would be arrested and charged with trespassing with the intention of stealing. No, she did not want anyone to come and accuse her of trespassing and end up in prison. It was only after her close friend, *Va*Margaret, whom she had come with to see the new house, had convinced her that the house really belonged to Herbert and Netsai, that cavernous *Va*Soda perched herself on one of the sofas with confidence.

*Va*Margaret was *Va*Soda's closest *sahwira*. A *sahwira* in Shona is a bosom friend whose friendship is beyond ordinary friendship and the bond between their families always develops into a strong kinship. Only a *sahwira* can say things ordinarily considered insulting or taboo without anyone taking umbrage. To someone not familiar with the relationship, when you listen to *sahwiras* talking to each other, you can almost think that a fight will break out, but no, it never happens because *sahwiras* are licensed to have unfettered talk.

"Don't you see the pictures hanging on the walls? There is your son Herbert and *muroora Mai*Farai," *Va*Margaret said, pointing at the photos. *Va*Soda relaxed.

That day Netsai left for home earlier because she had special visitors to attend to. Netsai wanted to make them as comfortable as possible. She wanted to give her *vamwene*; mother-in-law, a tour of the house. When Netsai got home, *Va*Soda even became more content that the house indeed belonged to her son and his wife.

After all the customary greetings were done between mother-in-law and daughter-in-law, and between Netsai and *Va*Margaret, *Va*Soda was jovial and thanked her son's ancestors by reciting his totem creed. Herbert's totem was Mufakose.

"Thank you, the great spirits of the Mufakose clan for guiding my son to buy this beautiful house," she shouted, jumping and, dancing.

"Soda, that's not enough. You also need to thank *Mai*Farai's ancestors, since their daughter has worked hard for this too!" *Va*Margaret told her friend.

"What difference does it make, Margaret? A married woman is recognized through her husband's name and ancestors. You have spent too much time as a nanny in those white suburbs. You seem to have forgotten our Shona customs," *Va*Soda retorted.

"You think her ancestors will be pleased? Buying a house is a momentous step and is only expected from middle-aged couples, not these young ones. This is a result of combined effort - *mushandirapamwe*. Every Shona person has his or her own totem, just like every fish which leaves its swimming trail in the waters," *Va*Margaret said.

Netsai realized that this could go on and on, because each time the two women chided each other, on-lookers expected it to become physical, but these two, would end up laughing and joking again. It was difficult for other people to take any side, because these two were *sahwiras*, real friends, who shouted at one another as much as they laughed with each other. They were like birds of the same feather, which flock together.

Netsai called the housemaid and asked her to serve drinks.

"You want to feed us like pigs? We just had tea a few minutes ago. Let us rest, eat a proper meal first, and then we will tell you which drinks we would like to have," *Va*Margaret said. Netsai took no offense.

"Thank you Gushungo! May the Gushungo spirits keep the river of blessings flowing your way! Keep up the good work...." *Va*Soda was using the wrong totem to address her daughter-in-law.

"Soda?" *Va*Margaret intervened, "Why are you mixing up *Mai*Farai's totem? Women of the River totem are known as *Mangwenya Mbwetete*, not Gushungo. That's the address for the male people of the River totem. You say I spent most of my time working for white people; you seem to be more confused than I am."

"I had completely forgotten. Blame it on the excitement," VaSoda said.

"It just shows that you hardly sing your daughter-in-law's praise totem," *Va*Margaret said.

Netsai just smiled. She had been married to Herbert long enough and they had children of school going age and it was embarrassing that her mother-in-law still did not know her totem well enough.

"Praising Netsai with her clan's male totem, Gushungo, is as good as vulgar, Soda. Don't you know that Gushungo means Tsiwo, and Tsiwo is equal to the female sex organ? The women of her clan totem are not praised as Gushungo but as MaNgwenya, Soda. Let me educate you!" VaMargaret said as a matter of fact.

"Thank you *Ma*Ngwenya, we praise the fruits of your hard work, *muroora*," *Va*Soda said, feeling embarrassed by the mix-up of the praise totems.

"What is there to say thank you for, *Amai*? It's us who should be grateful to you for inviting good luck into the family," Netsai politely said, clapping her hands together; a sign of gratitude. *Va*Margaret broke into a small ululation to complement the clapping.

"Now, these are the right manners, Soda. Next time do not chide me saying I worked too much on the white people's yards and lost my culture. You cannot teach me our Shona customs," *Va*Margret was talking while removing her cardigan at the same time. The house was very warm. She wrapped her cardigan around her waist, a style typical of most old Shona women.

"You could have given me your cardigan to put in the girls' bedroom, *Va*Margret?" Netsai asked.

"No, no, I would not want to forget my cardigan here when I go back. You know what you can do for me? Give me that drink you wanted to give us, but please make sure it's a very cold, icy beer, the one *Babava*Farai drinks. Also give me one of his cigarettes," she said.

"When are you going to quit smoking cigarettes?" *Va*Soda asked her friend, not hiding her disapproval. They always argued about *Va*Margaret's smoking habit.

"What is the difference between smoking a cigarette and stuffing some snuff-tobacco in one's nostrils? Tobacco is tobacco, my dear. Have I ever stopped you from your habit of stuffing powdered tobacco in your nostrils?" *Va*Margaret retorted back.

"Why don't you eat *sadza* first, before any beer?" Netsai suggested.

"Yes, Margaret, eat *sadza* first and take beer as a wash-down...." *Va*Soda did not finish her sentence.

"What? Beer is an appetizer, and you need to take two to prepare your stomach for a proper meal. You think I will become an alcoholic like your deceased husband? Though you deny it, insisting his mistress poisoned him. Poor man."

Netsai's mother-in-law was upset by this remark, but just for a little while. Soon they were joking and teasing each other again.

"Isn't it nice to eat, take a sip, eat and take a sip from your beer, and not down it like water? As a former *yardy*-worker, I know these things. I am not like you, Soda, who thinks you know English customs by wearing that wide sun-hat on your head inside the house," *Va*Margaret teased her friend.

Netsai, who was laughing, decided to go into the kitchen to take a break from the funny oldies. Her mother-in-law was wearing a wide sun hat, the same hat she had worn at their wedding. She loved the hat because it brought back memories of her favourite son's wedding. Besides, her mother-in-law's dressing always left a lot to be desired. She would wear thick socks in summer with some tennis shoes.

Netsai brought more drinks before taking her mother-in-law and *Va*Margaret outside to view the garden and the outside of the house. They sat on the garden chairs, and by now the two old ladies were so drunk that they needed support to get back into the house. They left the following morning to go back to the rural areas.

* * *

With time Netsai bought a car, which even made it easier for her to conduct her business. Netsai was a jack-of-all-trades; going to South Africa and Zambia to buy and sell. She became a prosperous businessperson. She also bought a mini-bus to operate as a public taxi. She became one of the first local women to be in the public transport business.

The couple now had a lot of money coming in; from the sewing business, the mini-bus and from their other houses. Netsai and Herbert were enjoying their success. Their lives had significantly transformed, from rags to riches. They now had the luxury to eat takeaways, or go to hotels for meals. They could afford to visit holiday resorts, something usually associated with foreign tourists. During each trip, they took many family photos.

* * *

One day when Herbert's mother came to visit again, she was shown some of these photographs by her grandchild, Tariro. She took offence at the photos in which Netsai appeared in her swimsuit, and the ones in which she was publicly kissing Herbert, wearing tight shorts and sitting on Herbert's lap. A traditional woman when it suited her, *Va*Soda was not impressed. As far as she was concerned, a married woman was not supposed to display her body in public. She frowned.

Tariro was surprised to see that her grandmother's reaction had changed. Unbeknown to Tariro, her grandmother stole one of the photos and slipped it into her handbag. *Va*Soda, did not stay long after that. She took her belongings and went back to the rural areas. The housemaid was dumbfounded because *Va*Soda had initially planned to spend a whole week. Herbert and Netsai returned from work to find her gone.

Netsai wondered if she had done something to anger her mother-in-law, or if it was Tariro who had said something to prompt her grandmother to leave so suddenly.

From then onwards, *Va*Soda boycotted Herbert's house and only came when there was something really special. The next time she visited was when she was told that Netsai and Herbert had a new baby girl, Rutendo. She came to visit when the child was six months old. Even when she was being shown the new baby girl, it was obvious that she was holding a grudge against Netsai. Her grudge was inflamed when she saw Herbert kissing Netsai and giving her a bouquet of roses. She nearly choked with rage. She interrupted them by asking Herbert a question, "Why is this child different from the others? She is lighter than the others."

"What about you *Amai*? Aren't you the light one in the family?" Herbert asked his mother. "Your granddaughter has your complexion."

"Even though I have a light complexion, I am not as light as this one," *Va*Soda said, trying to sow a doubt on Rutendo's paternity

"Your friend, *Va*Margaret always tells us that our father was attracted by your light skin," Herbert reminded his mother.

"You can't possibly believe everything Margaret tells you," *Va*Soda said although she knew her friend was right.

"Why did you leave your friend this time around, *Amai*?" Herbert asked. He wanted to ease the tension in the room.

"You do not expect her to chaperone me all the time, do you?" *Va*Soda feebly protested and everyone laughed. Although Netsai laughed, she could see that there was something disturbing her mother-in-law. Netsai could not bring that up with her husband, to avoid him thinking she disliked his mother. The next day when they bought some groceries for the old woman to take back to the village, her mood lightened up a bit.

CHAPTER Four

Netsai's happiness in her new house was short lived. The honeymoon was soon over. Things between Herbert and Netsai changed on Rutendo's first birthday. Netsai had been planning to take the whole family to a hotel to celebrate Rutendo's birthday. Herbert did not come home on time, as he was expected to do. Netsai and the children waited eagerly already dressed in their Sunday best. The children soon gave up on waiting for their father. It was the first time Herbert had ever done such a thing. This worried Netsai and the children, and eventually they decided to eat the birthday cake without him. They sang the happy-birthday song for Rutendo, and the housemaid prepared a quick meal for the occasion. The children felt let down by their father. They had looked forward to eating at a hotel, and now they had to make do with a home-cooked meal.

By the time Netsai went to bed, Herbert had still not returned. She woke up in the middle of the night to breastfeed her baby, and was surprised to find Herbert's space on the bed still empty. There was no sign of Herbert. She checked the time, and realized that it was 3.00 a.m. At first she thought the bedroom clock was not working properly, but the clocks in the other rooms showed the same time. She became restless, paced the house, asking herself questions, and answering them at the same time.

"Maybe he was in an accident. Should I phone the police? No, maybe I need to give it a little bit more time. Maybe I should wait until tomorrow morning. Should I phone his older brother and tell him, but then it won't be nice to wake people this early. I will call them tomorrow if Herbert does not turn up."

Each time she heard the sound of a passing car, she looked through the curtains, hoping that it was Herbert's car. She was hungry and went into the kitchen to fix a snack. She found a pot with leftover food, which she decided to warm up on the stove. But she fell asleep on the kitchen stool, only to be awakened by a thick choking smoke. The food was burning

"Oh my God!" She panicked, running to the lounge, thinking that the house was on fire. After a while, she regained her composure and remembered that she had put a pot on the stove to warm up some food. Netsai walked back to the kitchen and removed the burnt pot from the stove, filled it with water and opened the kitchen and lounge windows for fresh air to fill the house. "Oh God, I nearly burned down the house. What's wrong with me? Am I losing my sanity?" Netsai was very disturbed by Herbert's failure to come home. It was the first time he had slept out since they got married.

If there is nothing wrong with him, then I wonder what happened. Can he be having a small house somewhere? Is this how it starts? Maybe I am wrong, rushing to conclusions. I am probably stressing myself for nothing. My blood pressure will shoot up and cause problems. But what could have happened, that could stop him from coming home on our daughter's first birthday? Netsai was restless and confused.

She sat down, her head resting on the chair, looking upwards at the ceiling. Eventually she decided to go back to the bedroom to sleep, but tossed and turned as she found it difficult to sleep. When she did fall asleep it was already morning. She woke up to get ready to go to her dressmaking shop. She wanted to rush to work and open the doors for the assistants to get in, but remembered that one of the girls had a key to the main door and so decided to take her time to prepare.

When she went into the lounge to get the clock she had left there the previous night, she was surprised to find someone sleeping on the sofa. She realized it was Herbert when she saw his shoes. She was stunned. She pulled the quilt from him, and he mumbled something as he covered himself again.

"What is this, Herbert...?" Netsai asked, with fury.

"What is what?" Herbert was not in the mood to talk to Netsai. His eyes were red and puffy. He had been drinking.

Netsai left him. She went to help the maid to clean the house. She always helped the maid with housework so that the maid would have more time with the baby. The maid was also the nanny. Netsai then prepared the baby's feed, which she poured into thermal flasks to keep warm. She instructed the maid to lock the doors and firmly close the lounge doors.

"The man of the house is drunk today. I don't want the children to see him like that," she instructed.

"Okay, *Amai*, I will do as you say." The maid referred to Netsai as mother; a sign of respect, even though there was a small age difference between them. Her name was Tsitsi. She was a trustworthy and hard-working person who had worked for Netsai for so many years that Netsai now considered her a family member.

As soon as Netsai's car left the driveway, Herbert immediately got up from the sofa and went to sleep in the bedroom. Netsai, who had forgotten her wallet on their headboard, returned to the house to collect it. She found Herbert undressing, ready to get into bed. They looked at each other like two bullfrogs, Herbert's face signalling a don't-bother-asking-me-anything warning.

"What is this Herbert? You sleep out, and you don't even bother to explain what happened?" Netsai said, closing the door behind her.

"*Iwe mhani!* The car broke down on my way home. Did you expect me to carry it and bring it home? Hmmn?" Herbert asked, not hiding his agitation.

"You can tell me the car broke down without being so rough and cheeky!" Netsai was trying to be reasonable.

"Leave me alone. I want to sleep," Herbert said, getting under the quilt and pulling it over his head.

Netsai was really worried about this new Herbert emerging before her eyes. She took her wallet and left.

Thinking of Herbert made her angry. Something had happened to him. He was behaving like a heartless brute. She drove to work worrying about Herbert and nearly drove into another car.

When she got to her shop, the girls greeted her, but they noticed that Netsai was not as happy as on other days. She took out a pen and a notebook, but wrote nothing. One of the girls asked Netsai if she was not feeling well. Her mood was a cause for concern, because Netsai was usually chatty to her customers and her *girls*, and also cracking jokes most of the time.

And when she was not feeling well, Netsai always told the girls, but on this morning she did not say anything about not feeling well. The girls were worried. They could see that something was bothering their boss.

The pen fell from her hand and the noise it made on the concrete floor brought Netsai back to life, because she was dozing with a pen and paper in her hand. She went to the bathroom.

"What could be the matter with mama? I have never seen her this low," Yeukai, one of the girls said. She was the most senior of all the girls.

"It looks like there is something troubling her," Chipo answered.

"You think so? Maybe the baby is not feeling well, and was troubling her all night. Didn't you see she was falling asleep on the chair?" Eliza suggested.

"She would have told us. Mama is an open person. She always tells us if the children are not well," Yeukai was worried.

"You know...." Eliza did not finish what she wanted to say, because Netsai walked back into the room. Netsai collected all the finished dresses for delivery.

"After the delivery I am not coming back to the shop. I have a headache. Anyone who comes looking for me, just tell them I will be back on Monday. Don't forget to write new orders down, ok?" Netsai instructed, not looking anyone in the face, as if she was afraid that they would read her thoughts and see what was troubling her. At that moment, she felt as if the whole community and the whole country knew about her matrimonial problems.

"See you on Monday, and have a nice weekend," Netsai said, leaving.

"Same to you, mama," the girls chorused. They exchanged glances.

"Did you notice that her eyes were red and puffy? She was crying." The girls could not stop worrying about their boss.

"What can it be, *vasikana*, girls? Can it be that she was beaten by her husband? That is what many of us women go through in our homes. But her husband is a quiet man. That would be a first," Yeukai said. She had asked the question and answered it herself.

"There are too many problems in this world," Eliza responded to Yeukai's soliloquy.

"Too many problems indeed," Chipo echoed.

* * *

When Netsai left the shop for the quick deliveries, part of her mind wanted her to go home, but the other part decided it was better to go and tell her aunt, her father's sister, what was troubling her. She went to her aunt's, where she was received by her aunt's husband.

"What made you think of us today? Is everything alright? Why do you dislike me these days my junior wife?" *Va*Simon was Netsai's *Babamukuru* by custom she could also address him as uncle depending on how close they were. *Va*Simon called Netsai his junior wife because as was Shona custom, the man who married a girl's paternal aunt could inherit the niece upon the death of the aunt, or if the aunt turned out to be barren, the husband would be given one of his wife's nieces or sister as a wife.

"I always come here, but you are never home. I am very surprised to find you home today, what happened?" Netsai embraced her aunt's husband.

"You come when I am at work because you will not be coming to see me, but your aunt."

"Next time I will pass through your work place to announce my visit so that you can log me in your register." They both laughed.

"Do you want to end your visit at the gate, with your *Babamukuru*?" Netsai's aunt, *Tete*Susan, called from the house.

"It seems your aunt's jealous. She thinks you will snatch her husband," *Va*Simon said.

"Feeling jealous for an old man like you? Leave me alone. Would Netsai want to be in the company of an old man like you?" *Tete*Susan joked.

"Oh, that's what you think! Women still find me attractive," *Va*Simon said, taking Netsai into the house, they were walking hand-in-hand.

"Even if you walk hand-in-hand like two love-birds, I will call Herbert here, and we will see what happens." They all laughed again.

"I can see you are jealous." *Va*Simon addressed his wife. Once in the house, Netsai told them the purpose of her visit.

"Aagh, you are jealous. What do you want Herbert to do when you are still '*thin*' (fragile after giving birth)?" *Va*Simon joked. *Thin* was rhetoric for a woman who was breastfeeding, and had just had a baby, so her husband was not expected to make love to her.

"*Babamukuru*, I am not laughing or joking. How can I be fragile when Rutendo is a year old? Can I still be called a fragile woman? Some babies of her age have already stopped breastfeeding."

*Va*Simon and his customary *junior wife* had a close relationship; they teased, argued and laughed together.

"You want him to make you pregnant again? Will that be an accident again, like you said when you were pregnant with this baby?" 'It was an accident *Babamukuru*', you talk about accident as if it was a collision of two cars on the road? A new baby will ruin your chances to work for yourself, and now you want to know everything that he is doing. He will make you pregnant again and we will see what will become of you and your business," *Va*Simon said. "Where do you come from Netsai, where people don't know that there is contraception?" He said. "Now that you...." *Va*Simon did not finish because his wife interjected

"*Va*Simon, I can see you are the jealous one. But jokes aside, you know what my niece; people can drink beer the whole night. Is it not the first time he has slept out? Then forgive him." Aunt Susan did not want to put salt on an already bleeding wound.

"And the fact that he has never done it before makes it more worrying." Netsai added after explaining the details of the previous night.

"Don't worry too much, men always do that. Even your *Babamukuru* here, *Va*Simon, I ended up asking *Ma*Gumede, the shebeen queen, to give him a blanket each time he overstayed at the drinking party," *Tete*Susan tried to cheer her niece.

"You think I don't know that Netsai inherited her jealousy from you. Did you mean it, that *Ma*Gumede should give me a blanket to sleep in her house?" *Va*Simon said. They all laughed.

"I don't know what to make of it, *tete*, but Herbert has really changed. I don't even know what to expect when I get back home. This morning he was behaving like a wounded tiger ready to attack."

"You were taking Herbert for granted. Let him teach you a lesson and remind you of his rightful position," *Va*Simon said, drawing smoke from his tobacco pipe.

"*Babamukuru*, where have you seen people smoking indoors? You are choking us," Netsai said, coughing.

"So you now want to vent your anger and frustration on me? Let me stop smoking so that when you choke from your anger you will not have me to blame," he replied.

"I don't take your jokes seriously," Netsai said, shaking her head.

"Do as I told you," *Tete*Susan said, referring to the Herbert issue.

"I have seen you *tete*, let me rush home to breastfeed the little girl."

"Can you drop me in town as I want to collect my car from the garage?" *Va*Simon said as he put on his jacket.

On the way to town, Netsai forgot about her problems for a short while, because her *Babamukuru* was entertaining her with his endless jokes all the way. He was a humorous person. *Va*Simon reminded Netsai about Ernest, her high school boyfriend. Ernest was now living and working overseas, and he was *Va*Simon's favourite. When Ernest came to Harare on one of his visits, he had bumped into *Va*Simon at his work place where he had come to pick up something. He left his overseas address with *Va*Simon, hoping that Netsai would keep in touch.

"If Herbert bothers you too much, you can always go back to Ernest." Netsai laughed at the suggestion.

"You know, there are some people whose love does not die. I remember how you ill-treated Ernest because of this Herbert of yours. I still believe that when he came to my workplace he wanted to find out how you were getting on. He genuinely loved you, and still does."

"I don't know," Netsai responded.

"Ernest loved you from when you were still in secondary school, till he went to the university. I have never seen anyone genuinely in love as he was."

* * *

Years back, when Netsai was in Form 3, Ernest was doing Advanced level, in Upper 6. He was the school head boy. When he went to university, Ernest visited Netsai regularly at the school she was attending. Everyone in the community knew about their relationship. Netsai did not pass her Ordinary level exams very well, so she spent one more year at home repeating the subjects that she had failed. Ernest helped her with those subjects, especially Accounts and Mathematics. Ernest was studying towards a Bachelor of Arts in *Business Studies* degree at the University of Zimbabwe. Netsai eventually passed the subjects she re-wrote and enrolled for a *Secretarial Course*, while Ernest was finishing his third and final year at the university.

They were intending to get married the year after Ernest finished university, and Netsai her Secretarial studies, but not everyone was happy about the two. One of the girls in the community began to spread rumours that she too, was seeing Ernest, and went out of her way to get a photograph taken with Ernest in compromising poses. What she did not tell people was that she was just friends with Ernest, and when Ernest posed for the photos with her, he saw nothing wrong with hugging her. Netsai had not been pleased, even though Ernest tried to explain to her that Rose was making up everything. Netsai decided to break up with Ernest.

* * *

"But what exactly made you decide to break up with Ernest? Was it just about Rose? Or you were already seeing Herbert? What attracted you to Herbert? Was it the company Benz he drove around?"

"Today you are really on my case, *Babamukuru*," Netsai complained.

"He lied to you that it was his own car, hmm? Did he? And the guy is still what he was then, a poor driver. I know you have tried to improve him by encouraging him to further his education, I am sorry, but that man of yours is thick headed. A raw person is a raw person, now look at the life Ernest is leading, superb life!"

Netsai just laughed, shaking her head. She too, knew that her *Babamukuru* was right, but did not want to admit it.

"If you want his address, I can give it to you."

"What would I do with it, *Babamukuru*? Leave me alone."

"You have certainly tried your best to help build Herbert's life, trying to improve his status among other men, but some people, *amainini* are really thick."

"*Babamukuru*, don't make me laugh more than I am already doing now," Netsai said, laughing even more.

"I don't know my *junior wife*, why you couldn't see the difference between Herbert and Ernest. Even though they say love is blind, but you can see the difference now. Don't you? Maybe love blinded you." They laughed till their eyes watered with tears.

"If Herbert hears you say all these things about him, hey?"

"Where is Herbert now? Have you forgotten what he did to you, or you were only playing with us?"

The distance to town became short because of VaSimon's humour, so much so that after a few minutes they were in the city centre. After dropping VaSimon near the garage he was going to, Netsai was now thinking of what lay ahead. She wondered whether to park the car somewhere, or to go home. She drove home instead.

When she got home, she was told that Herbert had just left.

Herbert did not come back home that night, nor in the morning as Netsai had hoped for.

For the whole week Herbert did not come back.

Netsai woke up as usual and went to work as if nothing unusual was happening to her life.

Later the following week, Netsai returned home to be told that Herbert had come to the house in the afternoon. When Netsai opened the wardrobe to get some clothes to change into, she noticed that some of

Herbert's clothes were missing. Netsai felt like she was dreaming, and sat on the edge of the bed, wondering what was happening. For another week Herbert did not come home. He now appeared for a day or two and disappeared again. Netsai didn't know whether to confront him or to just observe quietly. She eventually summoned her courage and confronted him.

"Herbert, how can you spend the entire week away, from home, not telling me where you are? I phoned your work place and they told me that you are on leave. What is happening?"

"I went to the village," Herbert snapped, avoiding Netsai's eyes.

"Without even telling your older brother?" Netsai questioned.

"Am I a small boy to tell my big brother everything I do?" Herbert was getting agitated.

"Tsitsi, can you prepare *sadza* for me!" Herbert called out to the maid, as he opened the newspaper and browsed through it. Netsai could see that their life was changing. She was looking at a different Herbert from the one she had married more than a decade ago.

"Do you think what you did was right? To just go away like that without letting me know?" Netsai was angry.

"I am reading the newspaper, my friend. Don't disturb me," Herbert said, as if he was talking to a nobody and not his wife.

"Is there any need to be rude?" Netsai was getting angrier, too.

"If you keep irritating me, I will move out of this house, do you hear me? Don't bother me. You are used to treating me as one of your employees at the shop and not the head of this house!" Herbert was talking in a raised voice, his eyes bulging with anger.

Netsai went into the bedroom. She began to cry, but wiped her tears when Farai came into the bedroom.

"Mum, where was dad this past week?" Farai asked his mother, concerned with what was happening to their once happy family.

"He had gone to the village," Netsai replied, avoiding her son's gaze. Farai noticed that his mother had been crying.

"He is lying...." Farai did not finish what he wanted to say because his mother cut him short and reproached him for what he had said.

"It's wrong to say your father is a liar, Farai!"

Farai left the bedroom in a huff and went back into his room to do his homework. Farai knew of his father's extra-marital affair, everyone in his school knew about it. Tsitsi finished preparing supper and called the family to eat. Farai looked at his father with hate-filled eyes, and felt his stomach churn. He stood up, left the table and went back to his room to continue with his homework. That night, supper was not the usual happy meal affair filled with conversation and laughter. Netsai just picked on her food. The mood was worse than at a funeral meal. Mourners do chat, even though in low tones.

CHAPTER Five

After the confrontation between Netsai and Herbert, Herbert stayed at home for more than a week, coming home early and spending time with his wife and children. Netsai was almost convinced that everything was now backing to normal. When he told her that he wanted to spend some of his annual leave days in South Africa, where he also wanted to buy some spare parts for his car, Netsai did not object. She, too, wanted South African rands, which she knew he would bring her. He stayed for a week in South Africa, and when he returned, he brought presents for his children, and the South African rands that his wife wanted. When Herbert gave her a small amount of just R200, she did not know whether to get angry or not, but eventually she decided that half-a-loaf was better than nothing. The R200 would be enough to buy food on her next trip to South Africa, she decided.

"Thank you for the money. It will be enough to buy food on my next trip", she said.

"I want to sleep for a while, I am tired from driving," Herbert spoke as he got up from the sofa to go to the bedroom.

That week Herbert stayed at home. He went to work and came home straight afterwards, like he used to do.

* * *

At the end of the month Netsai decided to go and collect rentals from the lodgers in their two houses. She went to their old house first in Glen View, before going to Milton Park. When she arrived at the house, she found her old friend *Mai*Chido, who was in charge of all the other lodgers, at home.

"It seems like both you and *Babava*Farai, were missing us today, to come here one after the other! It's definitely going to rain, because it's unusual for

*Babava*Farai to come here," *Mai*Chido said, embracing Netsai.

"Ah, was he here as well?" Netsai was surprised.

"He came to collect money for rent so that he...." *Mai*Chido did not finish. Netsai interrupted her before she finished what she wanted to say.

"You mean he collected the rentals?" Netsai said slowly with a confused voice. She did not want to let *Mai*Chido know that she did not want Herbert to collect the rentals, but *Mai*Chido had already noticed it, from Netsai's reaction, that all was not well, and that she had made a huge mistake.

"*Amai*Farai, wasn't I supposed to give your husband the money? I can see you are not happy with that at all," she said.

"No, not really, it's just that he did not tell me he was going to collect the money," Netsai, tried to reassure *Amai*Chido so that she would not feel guilty for what she had done.

"*Shamwari,* I have stayed with you long enough to know that you are not happy. What is really happening?" *Mai*Chido was concerned about her friend.

"I will come back some other time so that we can sit and talk. But please, can you do me a favour, next time when he comes, tell him that you have already given me the money."

It was obvious that Netsai was stressed, that she wasn't her usual self. Something was happening in her life. Netsai did not waste any more time, and decided to go to Milton Park, where she found *Amai*Mandy, the tenant, at home as well.

"How are you my friend? Did you bring my order? I gave *Babava*Farai the sizes and measurements the other day," *Amai*Mandy asked.

"What order are you talking about?" Netsai didn't know anything.

"*Babava*Farai didn't tell you? He came here yesterday to collect rentals," *Amai*Mandy clarified.

Netsai kept quiet. She felt as if she was running out of breath, like someone was chocking her.

"Are you alright, *Amai*Farai?" *Amai*Mandy asked.

"I think I am coming down with a soar throat," Netsai said, faking a cough.

"It's very windy. The weather is changing everyday," *Amai*Mandy said.

"I think *Babava*Farai forgot to tell me. What was the order?"

"I want some clothes for a wedding."

"I am going to South Africa next week. I will bring them for you."

"That would be great." *Amai*Mandy was delighted. She gave Netsai details for her order, and Netsai only responded by nodding her head all the time. It was obvious something was *eating* her soul.

"The big tree at the back, was it finally removed?" Netsai inquired, going to the back of the house to inspect, because the tree's roots were spreading under the main house, threatening to cause some damage to the house. When she finished her inspection, she informed *Amai*Mandy that she was leaving.

"I am going, *Amai*Mandy!" Netsai shouted.

"I will come and see you off," *Amai*Mandy called back.

"Don't worry, I am running late," Netsai said, walking to her car. They waved at each other, and Netsai sped towards the city. Her mind was disturbed.

"My husband has changed. What is really happening, to him? What ever it is that has come into my house is too big to be controlled." Netsai realized it was getting dark and decided to go home.

When Rutendo saw her mother, she ran towards her. Netsai picked her up

"Is your daddy home, Rutendo?" Netsai asked as she kissed the child on both cheeks.

"He is in the bedroom, sleeping," Tariro answered, relieving her mother of the bag she was carrying. "How was your day, mum?" she went on.

"I had a good day, my love. Have you done your homework already, now that you are watching television?" Netsai asked her daughter.

"I finished it a while ago, mum," Tariro replied.

Netsai sat down and began to breastfeed the toddler. When she finished, she went into the bedroom to put Rutendo in her cot bed. Herbert was fast asleep, and it was almost 7 o'clock in the evening. Netsai looked at the clock and at Herbert. She was surprised that he was snoring, at that time of the evening. She wanted to wake him up, so that they could talk, but Netsai decided against the idea. She went back to the lounge to sit with her kids and watch television. The children left to go to their rooms to sleep, leaving Netsai watching television on her own. She fell asleep on the sofa and was woken up by Herbert when he brought Rutendo, who was crying for her breastfeed.

"I have been trying to wake you up for a long time. Didn't you hear Rutendo crying?" Herbert spoke while putting Rutendo on Netsai's lap.

"I had fallen asleep," Netsai replied, holding Rutendo so that she would not fall on to the floor.

As Herbert returned to the bedroom, Netsai called him back.

"*Babava*Farai, can I have a minute with you?"

"What is it? I want to sleep!" Herbert answered, coming back into the lounge. Netsai waited for him to sit down.

"What is it?" Herbert asked, standing up. It was obvious that he did not want to sit down.

"Can't you sit down? What kind of sleep is it, after all, you went to bed before seven?" Netsai asked, trying to be conciliatory.

"What is it that you want to discuss in the middle of the night like this?" Herbert asked, sitting on the sofa.

"I wanted to know about this month's rentals. When I went for collection today, I was told that you had collected the money already. What is really happening?"

"From today onwards, I will be collecting all the money from the lodgers. Do you hear me?" Herbert spoke as he got up to return to the bedroom. He was demonstrating to Netsai that he was the man of the house.

"Just like that? Are we not supposed to sit down and discuss family issues before you make unilateral decisions? You are just doing your own things. What has got into you?" Netsai was visibly angry.

"You used to bully me around, that's over!" Herbert said, almost shouting as he walked back to the bedroom.

"Did you deposit the money into the bank" Netsai wanted to know.

"Don't ask me silly questions!" Herbert shouted banging the bedroom door, leaving Netsai dumbfounded.

CHAPTER Six

Herbert woke up as if nothing had happened the previous night. He put on a very expensive suit, which he had bought in Johannesburg, and prepared to go to work as usual. Netsai was busy helping Tsitsi with the housework and preparing the children for school. There was tension between Herbert and Netsai, who were behaving like two bullfrogs, hostile towards each other. When Herbert left, he did not bother to say goodbye to his wife. He bolted out of the door and went straight to his car. Farai and Tariro, who were usually dropped at school by their father, had to run after him when Herbert was reversing the car in the driveway, ready to leave.

It was unusual of him to leave the kids, and Netsai and the maid just exchanged glances. Herbert always left home at 7.00 am, but that day he decided to leave thirty minutes earlier.

"Farai has left his sandwiches behind. I will take them to the car," Tsitsi said, picking the lunchbox and running towards the car.

"Farai, you have forgotten your sandwiches!" Tsitsi called out, giving Farai the lunchbox.

"You are an idiot, boy! You want me to be late for work, isn't it?" Herbert shouted.

He was angry. Tsitsi was stunned. She stood near the car, in disbelief.

"I had forgotten the lunch *Baba*," Farai said, fear registered in his voice. He was afraid of his father.

"I forgot! I forgot! What kind of forgetting is that? You behave like a zombie! Are you crazy boy?" Herbert was shouting at the top of his voice as he drove out of the driveway, onto the street.

"Daddy! I forgot my homework on the bed!" Tariro said, opening the door to go and fetch her homework.

"What did you say? Get out of my car, both of you! Get out. Now! You spoilt children! You will take a bus

to school. Your mother is not raising you properly!"
Herbert shouted.

Farai and Tariro jumped out of the car, puzzled by
their father's temper. Netsai called Farai and Tariro
back into the house, where she gave them their tea,
which had been disrupted when they rushed to their
father's car. The children were disturbed by their
father's raging temper and found it hard to drink their
tea. Netsai took them to school in her car instead.

* * *

When Herbert left the children, he was elated because
he had not wanted them to interfere with his plans. He
decided to pass through Aida's sister's place, where he
had not been for a few days.

"Welcome *Babamudiki*. Since you came back from
South Africa you haven't been to see us," Aida's sister
said, greeting Herbert.

"I had many pressing things to do, *Maiguru*,"
Herbert replied. Herbert was instantly jovial, as if he
had not been ranting and raving a few minutes before.

"I want to thank you for the present you bought me
in South Africa. Aida tells me you had a memorable
time together."

"It was just a holiday. We need to relax now and
again, *Maiguru*."

"For a business person like you, you need to enjoy
yourself, *Babamudiki*."

"You are right."

"Before we get carried away, I want to thank you for
the Rands. Thank you for all your help."

"Were they enough, *Maiguru*?"

"*Babamudiki*, if I am not grateful for something like
this then I will be as good as a witch, as our elders say.
One thousand rands is a lot of money. Even a witch
would be grateful for something like this," Aida's sister
said, clapping her hands to express her gratitude.

"Where is Aida?"

"She went to our parents' house in Highfields yesterday."

"I wanted to take her to work today."

"Sorry, she is not here."

They were silent for a few minutes, before Herbert told Aida's sister about his future intentions.

"*Maiguru*, I am planning to marry your sister," Herbert said. Aida's sister laughed.

"I am not joking at all, *Maiguru*. I am dead serious," Herbert said, and continued, "You don't seem to take me seriously. Anyway, I will discuss the matter with *Babamukuru*, your husband, so that he can arrange a *munyai* (middle-man)." Herbert sounded serious.

"*Babamudiki*, why do you want to talk about things like that so early in the morning? You make me laugh. This week, my husband is not around. He went away on a work trip."

"If *Babamukuru* arranges a *munyai*, I will go straight ahead and pay lobola." Herbert said, while at the same time pulling a wad of money, Z$2000, from his wallet and handing it to Aida's sister saying, "Give this money to Aida, please."

"Thank you, *Babamudiki*. I will give her." Aida's sister said, clapping her hands before she received the money.

"Let me rush to work, *Maiguru*." Herbert said, walking towards his car.

"You are now leaving on an empty stomach, *Babamudiki*."

"It doesn't matter, *Maiguru*. I will come and eat some other time."

* * *

After Netsai dropped the children off at school, she went home to search for the money, which Herbert had collected from their two houses. She searched the wardrobe, removing all the clothes and piling them on the bed and went through every pocket. She looked everywhere she thought Herbert could have possibly hidden the money, but could not find anything. She was behaving like a possessed woman. She was sweating with fury. She was also crying. Her knees buckled and she sat on the edge of the bed. She looked like a lizard basking in the sun. She was in a mental turmoil. After she regained her composure, she continued her search again, this time examining even the hems of Herbert's jackets and trousers. After a very long search and after turning everything in the house almost upside down, she came across their joint account bankbook.

She opened the book slowly as if it was a delicate thing, and her eyes opened wide in disbelief. Herbert had recently withdrawn *ten thousand dollars.* She dropped the book on the carpet, as if it was burning her hands. She opened her mouth as if to say something, but no words came out. She stood up and paced around the room, muttering and crying. No one came to comfort her. She dropped on the heap of clothes. She took the bankbook again, checking to see if the money collected from their two houses had been deposited into the account, but nothing had been deposited.

She thought that maybe Herbert had deposited the money into the other account, and began looking for the other bankbook. She checked for the book under the bed, between the base and the mattress, and nearly hurt her back when she removed the big mattress from the bed. She checked in the side drawers of the bed, but she did not find the book. She hurt her finger during the process, but did not feel any pain at all because the emotional pain she was feeling in her heart was more than the physical pain on her finger. The finger was bleeding. She went into the en suite bathroom and looked for the book in the tiny cupboards meant for toiletries and medicine. There was nothing. There was another tiny cupboard where they kept spanners and other tools, but she found nothing.

She returned to the bedroom where she sat on the base of the bed. That's when she realized that her finger was bleeding, and she took the tissue box on the bedside. There were very few tissues left in the box. She dipped her hand in the box to fish out a tissue, and her fingers felt something, and it turned out to be the bankbook she was looking for. Her heart began to beat faster, she didn't know what to do, whether to open the book or to just leave it. She opened it slowly, trying to protect herself from what she expected to see in the book. She opened the book and immediately, her head started spinning.

"*Yowe! Yowe!*" she cried. Netsai slumped on the floor with a thud. If anyone had seen Netsai at that moment, one would have concluded that she was a mentally ill intruder who had broken into someone's house. Her eyes were bulging as if she was face to face with a lion in the jungle with no room to escape. Her hair was untidy; the rollers that had been neatly put on earlier on looked like toy-spikes. Some rollers were still holding her hair firm, while others were loose and hanging on thin strands of hair. She began to pull them from her head; plucking them out as if plucking feathers from a chicken.

"Where did Herbert put all that money? Whatever has entered into my house is certainly too big for my little boots," Netsai muttered as she put the clothes that were scattered all over the bed back into the wardrobe. When she finished, she sat on the bed, with one hand supporting her chin. She was distressed.

Tsitsi knocked on the bedroom door, but Netsai didn't bother to respond. She called out to Netsai.

"Are you in, mama?" Tsitsi asked. The question brought Netsai back from the world she was in.

"Is it you, Tsitsi?" Netsai responded with a question. "I was dosing," she said, wiping tears off her face.

"I brought the baby, I think she wants to breastfeed now," Tsitsi said, standing at the door.

"Come in, bring her," Netsai said.

Tsitsi got in the bedroom and found Netsai squatting on the carpet. The room was a mess, with things tossed everywhere as if someone had just moved in and hadn't had time to sort things out. Tsitsi passed the baby to Netsai. She didn't understand what was going on.

"Are you ok mama?" she asked, worried about her employer.

"I am alright. It's just a headache," Netsai responded. Tsitsi had already noticed that all was not well.

"Your headaches are becoming too much, mama. Why don't you go and see a doctor?"

Tsitsi was worried about Netsai's well-being and marriage. She knew there was something troubling Netsai that was more than a mere headache.

"I took some pills. I will wait and see if they can help," Netsai replied, unbuttoning her blouse so that she could put Rutendo on the breast.

Do you want me to prepare something for you to eat before I do the laundry?"

"Go ahead with your laundry. I will prepare the food myself when I am ready because I don't think I am going to work today. I feel as if one of my veins is going to burst anytime." Netsai's eyes were puffy and red, making it believable that she might be having a migraine, but her eyes still did not disguise the fact that she had been crying as well.

"Go to a doctor, mama," Tsitsi repeatedly advised as she left the room, closing the door behind her.

She stood outside the room for a little while, talking to herself.

"Things change so fast. It's like a bad dream to think that this was one of the happiest families. Lord have mercy!" She then went to empty the laundry basket in the bathtub where she did the laundry.

Tsitsi realized that they were out of laundry soap and went to remind Netsai. That month Netsai had not done her regular monthly shopping because she did not have enough money. Netsai advised Tsitsi to use another kind of soap, the *chimugondiya* blue bar to scrub the clothes and boil some of the same soap for soft clothes.

* * *

Farai realised that he had forgotten his basketball trainers. He was not sure if he had left them in his father's car, or if they were in his room or in his mother's car. He became sad as the thought of his trainers brought back memories of what had happened in the morning that day. His basketball teacher noticed that something was troubling Farai.

"*Michael Jordan* what's up?" The teacher asked Farai, who they nicknamed after the American star. The teacher patted Farai on the shoulder. "Is everything alright, Farai?" the teacher asked with concern.

Farai just shook his head in response, signalling that all was not well.

"What's the matter?"

"I forgot my trainers at home. I am not sure exactly where they are."

"Don't worry. Since you wear the same size as me, I can lend you mine for today."

"Thank you, sir," Farai politely responded.

His performance that day was disappointing. The teacher could see that it was not only about the trainers, but that there was something else worrying him. His friends were also grumbling that he was letting the team down.

"Farai, you let everybody down today. What's wrong? " Some of the spectators asked him. Even his best friend asked him the same question.

"What was wrong with you today, Farai?"

"I have got a terrible headache," Farai said, looking at the ground.

Their teacher arrived.

"You were a disappointment, Farai. What's the matter?"

"I'm not well sir. My head is aching. I am sorry sir for failing you," Farai responded, avoiding his teacher's unforgiving look.

"You better go and rest. Tomorrow first thing, go to a doctor," the teacher said, patting Farai on the shoulder.

"I will do that, sir."

Farai walked from the sports ground with his friend and went to wait for his mother at the main school gate. He waited for quite a while before his mother came to pick him up, and when he got into the car, he broke down.

"What is it Farai? Are you crying because I came late to pick you up?"

Netsai was holding Farai's hand and massaging it gently. Farai did not reply. He continued to sob.

"Why are you crying, Farai? Tell mama, what's bothering you?"

"My head is sore and so I did not play basketball well. Our team lost." Farai was wiping tears from his cheeks as he spoke.

"Ah, is that why you are crying? You will play better next week. I will give you some paracetamol when we get home." Netsai drove away and then stopped at a service station where she bought some cold drinks. They were at the service station for a while.

As Netsai's car turned into the main road leading to her house, she saw Herbert's car in front of them, on his way home. When Herbert parked his car in the garage, Netsai was also driving into the yard and they got into the house one after the other. When Herbert saw his wife and son, he started shouting at Farai.

"Farai, you make us buy expensive trainers saying you need them for basketball when you don't even play the game. It is now clear that you are an expensive liar?" He was fuming.

"I play basketball dad," Farai responded softly.

"You said you can't play basketball without your trainers, so tell me, how did you play basketball today when you left them in my car?" Herbert poked Farai on the forehead.

"I forgot them, dad, when you asked us to leave the car because...."

Herbert interjected, "You want to put the blame on me? You are a spoilt brat, to make us buy expensive things when you don't use them. You like wasting our money!"

"I played basketball today dad, but I borrowed my teacher's trainers."

"Stupid!"

Farai did not know what else to do. He was afraid of his father. His mother, who had not said anything all along, called him to the bedroom. "Come and take some *paracetamol*, Farai, and sleep for a little while." Netsai took her son by the hand and led him to the bedroom, where she gave him two painkillers and took him to his room. She massaged his head since Farai was now crying. Netsai went back in to their bedroom where she began to sort out the clothes she had thrown about in the morning. She took her time sorting out the clothes, and Herbert followed her in the bedroom. He was all anger.

"Why do you make me look stupid when I am talking to the boy? You always do this foolish thing of taking his side?" Herbert was standing behind Netsai, but Netsai did not respond. She continued packing the clothes neatly into the wardrobe.

"Oh, so I am now a mad man who talks to himself? What kind of a house is it, where the mother and children do their own things? Is it still a family? That's why I am fed up of living here," Herbert said, as he went to sit on the bed.

Netsai turned her head to face Herbert, and gave him the bank account savings book, while saying, "So, it's me and my children who are doing their own things? Hmm! Can you tell me what you did with the Z$10,000, you withdrew from the bank?"

Herbert took the book and laughed. It was a provocative laugh.

"Is that why you turned the bedroom inside out? Shame on you woman! You know, as a man, you just don't tell your wife about every little thing that you do. I am a man, and I am entitled to do things with other men in private," Herbert spoke while putting on a jacket. He threw the savings book on the bed. Netsai was too angry to say anything. She just looked at him. Herbert went into the kitchen where he fetched a glass and poured himself water from the fridge.

"I have just set the table for supper, *Baba*," Tsitsi said when she realised that Herbert was about to leave the house.

"I am alright. I have got a headache. I am going to buy some painkillers in town," Herbert was fidgeting with his pockets, looking for the car keys.

When he found them, he bolted out of the house and drove away.

Tsitsi went to the bedroom to tell Netsai that supper was ready. She was still packing the clothes in the wardrobe.

"I am coming!" But she took a while before she came to the table.

"How is the headache, mama?" Tsitsi inquired after Netsai's health.

"It's much better, Tsitsi," Netsai replied, but her face was full of sadness.

"You are all complaining of headaches. What is wrong? I tried to wake Farai up for supper, but he said he has a headache too."

Tsitsi was worried about the 'headache plague', which had suddenly affected the whole family.

"Farai's headache started at school," Netsai said.

"Even *Baba* also said he has a headache. He said he was going to town to buy painkillers." Netsai just laughed and continued eating.

"I don't really know Tsitsi. Can you take Rutendo to the kitchen and feed her, please?"

"You are laughing, mama?" Tsitsi was perturbed.

"Why can't I laugh about it? Isn't this what they meant when they said people laugh at tribulations as if they are things to enjoy? Umm, *kuseka nhamo serugare*?" Netsai spoke while giving Tsitsi the baby to feed. "Can you please feed her, so that I can eat my food without being disturbed?"

"The relish doesn't have enough cooking oil. I used the last drops of oil we had in the house."

"It doesn't matter Tsitsi, you know I don't like having too much oil in my food. If there isn't enough cooking oil, you can always use butter instead."

"Even the butter, there is only a small amount left, enough for tomorrow, so I have kept it for the school children."

"That was thoughtful of you, Tsitsi." Tsitsi took the child and went into the kitchen. Netsai ate little, just enough so her breasts could produce milk for her baby since she was still breastfeeding. She was also worried about where she would get money to buy groceries since almost everything was nearly finished. She usually bought groceries with the rentals they got from their other houses. Tariro saw that her mother was worried, and was not eating much. She too became unhappy.

"Is your head still painful, mama?" Tariro asked her mother.

"It's better now, Tari."

"You are not eating, mama. What is the matter?"

"I have eaten what I was supposed to eat, Tariro," Netsai said.

She went to the kitchen and made a squash and took it to Farai's room.

"Leave it there, mama, I will drink it when I wake up," Farai was sleepy. Netsai decided to leave him, stood by the door for a while looking at her son, and switched off the lights before going to her bedroom to sleep.

Herbert returned home after midnight. He went to bed straightaway, but Netsai was still struggling to fall asleep, trying to imagine where and how Herbert had spent Z$10,000. She got up and left the room.

What is really happening with Herbert? Z$10,000 is not a small amount to just spend like that. Maybe he is going to tell me what he did with it, but still, I should ask him when the situation is alright. These days he is always angry and agitated. I doubt if something good will come out of this. I don't think he is up to any good. If I am ever going to feel any pain, this money has pained me, she thought. Her mind raced from one thing to another, before she eventually fell asleep on the sofa. She woke up in the morning and went to her bedroom to prepare to go to work.

Herbert was still lying in the bed but awake. He looked at Netsai from head to toe, as if sizing her up, before saying, "So, this is your new attitude? You run away from the bed when I come home. What's got into you?"

Netsai did not respond. Instead, she went to the wardrobe where she selected the clothes she wanted to wear that day, and went into the bathroom to have a bath. When she came back to the bedroom, Herbert continued.

"So, you don't want to talk to me any more? When I talk, you ignore me, who do you think you are? *Hee?*"

Herbert was angry. Netsai continued with her preparations for work. She wore the clothes she had selected from the wardrobe and began to apply some make-up. Herbert got up and went to sit next to Netsai.

"Didn't you hear what I just said?" Herbert spoke into Netsai's ear.

Netsai ignored him and continued with what she was doing. She picked her wallet, ready to leave. Herbert grabbed her hand with force. "Who do you think you are, woman?" Herbert was looking at Netsai in the eyes. Netsai showed him that she was not afraid of him and also looked him in the eye, not even blinking. "You think you are a man?" Herbert was now holding Netsai's hand in a firm grip.

"Leave me, Herbert. Leave me alone, do you hear me?"

She was trying to free herself from Herbert's tight grip.

"Herbert, Herbert. I am not your boyfriend!"

"Is it the first time I have called you Herbert?"

Netsai was still trying to loosen Herbert's grip. As a result she twisted her arm and yelled in pain.

"*Yowe-e, mai, yowe-e!*"

Netsai was squirming with pain, and as she was trying to *correct* the twisted arm. Herbert hit her in the face. She fell over the edge of the bed, and her face collided with the lampshade, smashing it. She began to bleed.

Netsai shouted at Herbert. She was angry.

"You are hitting me for wanting to know what you did with our money, which you withdrew without telling me. You collected money from the tenants and you did not deposit it in the bank. Is that why you are hitting me, hmm?"

Herbert kicked her.

"I will kill you, do you hear me!" He roared.

He was behaving like a brute possessed with demons. Farai, Tariro and Tsitsi ran to the bedroom and opened the door. Farai and Tariro began to cry when they saw their mother bleeding.

"Dad, please don't kill mama!" They chorused.

Herbert disappeared into the bathroom as if nothing had just happened. Tsitsi helped Netsai to stand up.

"Farai, Tariro, go to our neighbour *Amai*Chitapi and ask for a lift to school. You are going to be late. Run, Farai," Netsai told her children as she struggled to stand up.

Farai hesitated for a while, but his mother insisted.

"Run, please Farai, or you can call her and I will talk to her."

Farai ran to *Amai*Chitapi's and told her what his mother had said. She told Farai to get into the car, and drove to Netsai's house where she also had to pick Tariro up and drive them to school. On the way, *Amai*Chitapi drove past Netsai's car and realized that she was struggling to keep the car steady. *Amai*Chitapi stopped Netsai.

"Don't drive in this state, my friend. You could smash your car and get hurt or killed," *Amai*Chitapi was talking whilst taking Netsai's hand into her own.

"I have to go to the doctor, my friend."

"Get into my car and let me take you to your doctor before I take the children to school," *Amai*Chitapi suggested.

Netsai got into *Amai*Chitapi's car, and when the children saw her, they began to cry. *Amai*Chitapi consoled them by telling them that their mother was going to be alright since she was going to see a doctor. The kids cried even more. *Amai*Chitapi left Netsai at the doctor's surgery, and also gave her money for a taxi to return home. She continued to the school, and had to park the car for a while as she consoled the children who were still crying. She left them at the school.

After receiving treatment, Netsai took a taxi and went to the high-density suburb of Mufakose to her aunt's house. Her aunt was shocked when she saw Netsai bruised and swollen in the face like a bull that had been head butting an anthill. The bandage was still socked in blood.

Netsai explained what had happened.

"My niece, I am not happy with this. Herbert has made a serious mistake. He must understand that even though you are married to him, your head still belongs to us, he can have the legs." *Tete*Susan said while inspecting Netsai's wounds. "He married you for company and to get access to your legs, not your head," she was looking at the swollen eye.

"My legs and my head, my face, all belong to me, aunty," Netsai was angered by her aunt's old beliefs that a married woman must surrender her body to her husband.

"He paid *lobola*, so that he can do what he wants with your legs, but your head is ours. He has damaged it and he is going to have to pay us money to appease us."

"*Tete*, I want out of the marriage, I want a divorce. I am fed up," Netsai was breathing hard.

"*Muzukuru*, my niece, you surely don't want to end your marriage over something as petty as this. Don't you know that a husband and a wife are always fighting like siblings? We will talk to Herbert so that you can return to your house."

"I am no longer interested in him, aunty. If you accept any money for appeasement from him, he will make it a habit that he can beat me at will, then later pay."

"What has gotten into Herbert's head?" Netsai's aunt was puzzled by Herbert's violent behaviour.

"*Tete*, all along we were planning our things together as a couple, and now I am puzzled by his behaviour. What makes it worse is that he has also become violent. I can't stand his brutality. I am no longer interested in this marriage."

"To keep a marriage intact requires a lot of effort, my niece."

Netsai's aunt decided to call Netsai's mother so that she too, could help to talk Netsai into going back to her husband. Netsai's parents' house was in Marimba which was an affluent section of Mufakose. The house was a walking distance from where *Tete*Susan lived.

"*Vatete*, this is a bad spirit. Someone is sending bad spirits to Herbert for him to behave like this. These children have been living well, and all of a sudden they begin to fight," Netsai's mother said. She had not even embraced her daughter because when she saw the state Netsai was in, she panicked.

"You know, *Amai*, it is wrong for you to start talking about bad spirits when Herbert is doing this deliberately, and getting away with it."

Netsai tried to explain to her mother what had happened, but, her mother could not see any reason why Netsai could not go back to her husband. She did not understand how Z$10,000 could make someone break up her marriage. She began to draw parallels between Herbert and Netsai's father. She told Netsai about how her father had once left her for another woman, and how she had endured and waited for him to return.

She reminded Netsai of her ordeal, which was common knowledge to all the family members; how she had fought hard to save her marriage, played the good wife and patiently waited until her husband came back when he got tired of his mistress.

"Even though your father's former mistress opened shops with the money she expropriated from him, I am the ultimate winner because I am the one with your father, the one with a husband, while all she has to her name is just a business," Netsai's mother said. "What is more important is to be *Mai*Kudzingwa, to be referred to by your husband's name. Your father's former mistress established businesses, but her life is a void because at night when thieves come to rob her, she has no one to chase them away for her," Netsai's mother said.

Netsai explained to her mother that her father's former mistress would never need a husband to frighten thieves away because she had enough money to hire security guards to protect her business premises and her home. Her premises were always guarded. Netsai's mother argued that it was more important for a woman to have a husband than to have money and security guards.

"A man can go, can leave me, but I want my money which I worked hard for," Netsai told her mother. Netsai's mother was getting angry with her daughter, who was failing to understand why a man was more important in a woman's life than material things.

"Both money and a husband are necessary; money is needed for day-to-day living expenses, and a man is needed for company," *Tete*Susan tried to compromise, when she saw the rising tension between mother and daughter.

"Ha-a, *Tete*, a woman without a husband is empty, do not to beat about the bush. If you are not married, the society will not respect you, you become light like a piece of paper blown by the wind," Netsai's mother said.

"A person is respected by their deeds, not because they are somebody's wife," Netsai didn't seem to believe in the sanctity of marriage anymore.

"Netsai, you are now behaving as if you are talking to your friend. This is your mother you are talking to. What has gotten into you, *child*?" *Tete*Susan reproached Netsai. It was her first time to see Netsai as angry as she was. They knew her to be humble and quiet, but here she was, behaving like another person they did not know. Her aunt's husband, *Va*Simon, arrived from work and was surprised to see Netsai with a bandaged head and a swollen face.

"What happened, Netsai?" he asked, in shock.

Netsai shook her head and began to cry. She could not answer her *Babamukuru*, uncle.

"What is it, *Mai*Francisca? Why is Netsai bandaged like this?" he asked his wife.

His wife was quiet for a few seconds, before saying, "This is how Herbert is now repaying our trust with our daughter."

"He is a coward if he is beating up a woman. If he wants to fight, he must join a boxing club," *Va*Simon said.

"It's hard, *Babava*Francisca," Netsai's mother said, showing signs of fatigue.

"How are you *Amai*? I had forgotten about the greetings, especially with this," *Va*Simon said, greeting Netsai's mother, who, by virtue of Shona culture, was his mother-in-law since he could inherit Netsai or any of her sisters if something happened to his wife.

"I am well, if you are well, *Museyamwa*. We are faced here with this predicament that your *wife*, *Amai*Farai is in," Netsai's mother addressed *Va*Simon with his totem name, *Museyamwa*, because he was of the Eland clan. She was clapping her hands, at the same time singing his praise totem.

"What is Herbert trying to do, Netsai?" *Va*Simon was angry.

"Did I not come here to tell you that my home is in turmoil, and you said I was jealous?" Netsai reminded them.

"Just come back to me now, your customary husband. A long time ago cowards like Herbert were beaten in front of the village court with thick sjamboks. If he continues to behave like this, I will hire a muscle man to go and discipline him. *Mhonya chaiyo!* I am telling you," he said. Everyone laughed, as if all was well.

"I am not staying much longer, *Amai*, I left some unfinished tasks at work," *Va*Simon said as he fished for some money from his pocket, which he then handed to his wife. "This is money to buy my *Amai* some drinks, and buy my *junior wife* a beer, too. Are you still drinking beer, Netsai, or you are now afraid of your murderous husband?" *Va*Simon was trying hard to ease the tension in the house. He was always a humorous person. Netsai laughed before saying, "Ahh, I still drink, only that the medication I am on at the moment won't do well with alcohol."

Her aunt's husband left for work, and exited with his wife who was going to buy some drinks at a nearby tuck-shop, leaving Netsai and her mother alone in the house. Netsai's mother took the opportunity to inquire further into what had actually happened to Netsai.

"Netsai my daughter, for *Babava*Farai to hit you like this, what had you really done?"

"*Amai*, I no longer understand *Babava*Farai." Netsai was shaking her head as she spoke, tears trickling down her cheeks.

"Ah-ya-a!" Netsai's mother sighed, clasping her hands together. "Is this not because of your confrontational behaviour, my daughter? What did I tell you last time I saw you? Hmmn?"

Netsai did not respond. Her mother went on,

"It's all because you don't listen to us, elderly people, when we give you advise. You think you are a 'know-it-all', I don't know where that attitude will take you."

"*Amai*, if someone wants to change, they can just change. You can't do anything about it."

"You need to drive away the bad spirits haunting your house. You must go to church and to traditional healers to get good roots to drive them away," she advised.

"*Amai*, I can't do that."

"If you don't want me, your own mother, to give you advice, then who is going to do that? If it hadn't been for that traditional healer who lives near the egg market, *kuMazai uko*, do you think I would still be with your father today? You think life is a joke, Netsai!"

"*Amai*, I...." she gasped for breath before saying, "I...I can not take it anymore." Her aunt came into the house just then, back from the tuck-shop, and began to serve Netsai and her mother cold drinks. When she had finished having her drink, Netsai's mother prepared to go back to her house, but before leaving, she instructed Netsai's aunt to take Netsai back to her husband that very same evening and get Herbert's explanation of what had happened.

* * *

When Farai and Tariro finished their school activities for the day, they were picked up by *Amai*Chitapi and upon arriving home, they dashed to their parents' bedroom to check on their mother, but went back to the lounge crying.

"Where is mama, sisi?" They addressed Tsitsi the housemaid as *sisi*, because they took her for a big sister, and *sisi* was a synonym for housemaids as well.

"How did *Amai*Farai spend her day?" *Amai*Chitapi also asked.

"She hasn't come back home yet, since morning," Tsitsi replied, showing that she too was concerned about Netsai's absence.

"Has she been admitted into a hospital?" *Amai*Chitapi asked no one in particular, because she was worried. The mentioning of a hospital made Farai and Tariro to cry even more.

"Was mama admitted into hospital?" Farai asked *Amai*Chitapi as he took her hand into his.

"Mama is in hospital?" Tariro, too, asked. She was still crying.

*Amai*Chitapi hugged the children.

"Don't cry, children, your mother shall return home soon, don't cry. I am going to the hospital to check if she is there."

*Amai*Chitapi went to the hospital to inquire if they had admitted a patient with the name Netsai Kudzingwa. She was shown the admissions book, and saw that Netsai's name wasn't there. She went back to Netsai's house, and heard that Netsai had still not returned. She was by now very worried.

"If she comes back tonight, please let me know. Otherwise I will see you children tomorrow when I come to take you to school. If there is anything you require, don't hesitate to tell me, *sisi*, do you hear me?" *Amai*Chitapi said, turning to Tsitsi.

"I don't think there is anything we need at the moment. We are still ok." Tsitsi responded.

Meanwhile, Herbert was relaxing at Aida's sister's house, in the company of the sister, the sister's husband and Aida. They were drinking beer. There were loads of beers and other soft drinks on the table. They were consuming some *braaied* meat; all types of meat imaginable.

"So, what about my proposal to pay lobola, *Maiguru?*" Herbert resumed the issue he had raised with Aida's sister earlier that morning.

"I thought, *Babamudiki,* that it is wise for us to tell your blood-brother, because if we do our own thing without involving him, we may have problems tomorrow," Aida's sister said.

"If we do something like that, all my plans will be ruined. My brother is aware of the fact that my wife ill-treats me, but is always taking her side. It will not be easy for me to marry Aida otherwise," Herbert explained.

"Did you make an effort to explain everything that is happening between you and your wife to him?" Aida's sister wanted to get to the bottom of things.

"You think there is anyone who doesn't know about our problems? From the time we got married up to now, we have never had a good life. It's only that I was a person with a lot of patience."

"If what you told me of your relationship with your wife is true, I respect you young man., You are a strong and patient *young man.* Some women throw away good luck; to spoil such an opportunity, really? I cannot even bring myself to repeat what Herbert told me. This man has been strong, but it's only human to get tired, mate," *Va*Mungofa sided with Herbert. Aida was quiet. She did not know what to say.

"So, how do you want us to do it?" Aida's sister asked for her husband's opinion.

"It's easy to get a *munyai. Vano pera here?* They are numerous. We just look for one, and we go to pay the lobola. It's easy," *Va*Mungofa suggested.

"Next week I will go with you to Marondera to pay the *lobola.*" Herbert was still trying to convince Aida's sister of his intentions to marry her sister. When she confirmed that they were going to help, Herbert stood up and began to jump up and down with joy like a small boy who had just received a favourite toy. They sat down for a little while, enjoying their beers. Herbert left after watching the eight o'clock news bulletin. He was happy.

* * *

While Herbert was preparing to take another wife, Netsai's aunt was begging her to return to her home, but Netsai was adamant that she did not want to return to Herbert anymore.

"It's now almost 8 pm, and you are refusing to go back home, what do you want me to do, Netsai?"

"I am now terrified of living in that house with him, *tete.* You know, each time I think of going back there, my palpitations increase. I am scared, aunt, please let me stay here." Netsai was begging her aunt to let her spend the night at her house.

"If you don't want to return to your house, then I will have to take you to your parents' house. I don't want to be blamed tomorrow," *Tete*Susan said.

*Tete*Susan took Netsai to her parent's house. They walked in dead silence. The only sound that came from them was their footsteps. The atmosphere was tense. Although *tete*Susan was hesitant to take Netsai to her parents, she felt that she had no choice. Netsai felt going back to her house was like going to a prison. She knew that her parents were not going to accept her and would just send her back.

When they arrived they were received by Netsai's mother and *tete*Susan whispered to her, "I have brought the *child* home."

Netsai's mother pretended not to have heard and greated *tete*Susan in a lound voice. "*Pachipamwe, tete.* We see each other again," she said, looking at Netsai, disappointment registered in her eyes. Netsai's father emerged from their bedroom, and joined them in the lounge.

"Good evening my sister. Is everything alright for you to come at this time of the night? I see that you have your niece behind you, *Yowe!*" Netsai's father was shocked to see his daughter in bandages. His wife had not bothered to tell him what had happened to Netsai. She had hoped that by this time Netsai would be back at her house.

"There is nothing right, brother, as you can see for yourself. Netsai's story is a difficult one. I saw her coming to my house this morning, with a bandaged head as you can see. She said she was beaten by her husband. I tried to make her go back to her husband, but she refused, so I told her that she can not sleep at my house because I am too small for such a huge and heavy load. That is why you see us coming to you now," Netsai's aunt explained.

"My sister, how can your niece say she does not want to go back home, has she been divorced by her husband? Where is the *gupuro*, divorce token? I cannot accept her in my home if she has not been formally divorced. We all know that a divorced wife brings a *gupuro*, divorce token to her people. She is still someone else's wife and I can not have her back unless she has this token as evidence that Herbert doesn't want her anymore. If I take her into my home, tomorrow her husband can take me to traditional court and sue me for taking away his wife. Take her back. If her husband doesn't want her anymore, he knows our

custom, I need to see *gupuro racho, the* divorce token,"
Netsai's father was now angry. There was silence in the
room.

"But since she is afraid to go back home, why don't
you keep her for the night and if her husband still loves
her, he will come looking for her?" *Tete*Susan tried to
plead with her brother.

"I am not going to do such a foolish thing, sister.
Never! You see her mother still living with me here for
all these years, you think it was easy? It was not easy,
but she endured."

Netsai's father remained steadfast with his position.
He was a man who believed in his word and who did
not give in to pressure or persuasion.

"*Tete,* I am a well respected woman in our
congregation and one of my duties in my church is to
give marriage guidance to young couples, some who are
younger than Netsai and with more serious problems.
When you see how some of them have been battered by
their husbands, you wonder if they will survive. But
after counselling them, you see them leading happy
lives again. If there is anyone influencing her by telling
her that it's now fashionable to divorce husbands, then
she must go and live with those people, not in this
house! I don't want her here, *Tete.* I don't support
immorality. Never!"

Netsai's mother was preaching the gospel of
morality while her daughter was crying.

"You have heard for yourself, Netsai. Let me take
you back to your husband. Do you think he will harm
you if I take you to him? Let's go, you wouldn't want
your kids to grow up like orphans when you are still
alive, let's go." Netsai's aunt was now blackmailing her
niece, making her see the benefit of going back to her
husband and raise her kids herself. But Netsai
remained seated on the chair, as if she had not heard
what her aunt had said.

"Let's go, while the night is still young, my niece. If
we get home in good time, we might find your

Babamukuru still awake. He might be able to take us to your house in his car. If we find him in bed, it might be difficult to wake him up." Netsai rose up to go, but did not hide her displeasure about the whole arrangement.

"Let us pray before you leave," Netsai's mother said, kneeling down. Netsai gave her mother a meaningful look.

"God we thank you for this day we just ended. God in the universe, you are the one who made us see this day, from sunrise to sun set. God, our Father, we bring before you your servant, Netsai. Help her. Bless her. Bring the Holy Spirit into her house and drive away Satan from haunting her house. We curse all the demons, including their leader Belezebhuli, whom we chase out of Netsai's house now. My Lord, we bring before you Netsai's husband, so that you guide him and remove the violence in him, my Lord. And her children, we bring them before you as well, so that you can guide them. Make them one family living in harmony and togetherness. Make Herbert unconditionally love his wife, and Netsai to respect and humble herself before her husband, as it is written in your holy book, that a woman shall respect her husband, and a husband shall love his wife. We bring all this before you, Lord Jesus Christ, Amen."

When her mother and aunt were praying with their eyes closed, Netsai's eyes were wide open and she showed no interest at all in the prayer.

"Thank you *muroora*, sister-in-law, for the prayer. Let's go Netsai," *Tete*Susan said, urging Netsai to come with her. She did not want to waste more time at the house as it was getting late.

"Netsai, when your husband is angry, avoid confrontation. Go and live well my child." Netsai's mother offered last minute advice to her daughter.

*Tete*Susan and Netsai left. When they arrived at the house, they were told that *Va*Simon had not yet arrived home.

"What has delayed him today?" *Tete*Susan asked, throwing herself on the sofa because she was very tired. "Let's wait for him for a few minutes, if he does not turn up, we might have to take a taxi since it's getting very late."

Her aunt went into the bedroom and fetched a small box. She selected a few roots and put one type in an envelope and the other into a small plastic. She called Netsai who was sitting in the lounge, to come into her bedroom.

"Netsai-o-o!" she called. Netsai went to her aunt's bedroom, where she was gestured to the bed.

"Listen carefully; some of the people you see with stable families have to put extra effort in these happy marriages. This *muti*, love potion, in the plastic is for bathing so as to get rid of bad omen. This other one, you put under Herbert's pillow, Netsai's aunt explained to her how to use the *muti* she had given to her.

"Ah! *Tete*, you think if a man wants out of a marriage this *muti* can change him? I don't trust love potions." Netsai turned down her aunt's offer.

"He-e, Netsai! Give it a try and see what happens. You see all these stable homes standing and think people are not trying everything!" *Tete*Susan put the two packets into Netsai's hand. Netsai reluctantly accepted them, her aunt's husband arrived and Netsai and her aunt quickly hid their devious potions. Netsai's aunt did not want her husband to know that she, too, used love potions on him.

*Tete*Susan, switched off the lights in the bedroom and went to the lounge. *Va*Simon was surprised to see that Netsai was still at their house, but his wife explained why she had not gone. She asked him if he could take them to Eastlea.

"You want Herbert to beat me, thinking I was taking his wife from him?" *Va*Simon joked.

"Let's leave jokes aside, *Babava*Francisca. Let's go and leave the *child* at her house," his wife said with urgency.

"Child? You spoil her. Anyway let's go and leave this baby of yours. Your aunt spoils you, Netsai. Come, let's go little one!"

They arrived at Netsai's house and found Herbert sitting in the lounge. He greeted them with happiness.

"Welcome! Welcome!" Herbert said as he greeted Netsai's aunt and her husband. "Hi." He greeted Netsai with a cold voice. Netsai did not respond.

*Tete*Susan and her husband sat down on the sofas.

"How are you *Tete*, and *Babamukuru*?"

"We are well if you are well *Babava*Farai. How are you and the family?" *Tete*Susan inquired after Herbert and his family's health.

"We are all well."

"I don't see you at our *church* anymore. Which *church* have you joined now?" VaSimon asked.

Anyone listening to the conversation would have thought *Va*Simon was talking about a proper church, but *church* was street lingo for a pub. In the pubs they had their own bishops and *preachers*, those who drank more beer than others.

"These days I am going to other *churches*. *Ko, dzinopera here?* They are numerous. I will invite you to my new *church* soon. They sell the best wine," Herbert and *Va*Simon joked. They laughed. And after a brief pause, *Tete*Susan stated their main reason for coming to Herbert and Netsai's home.

"*Babava*Farai, as you see us in your house tonight, we saw *Amai*Farai come to our house today saying that you had a misunderstanding. So that is why we have come, to find out what it is that you have failed to understand between each other, which then led to the two of you to fight, nearly killing each other?" It was more of a question than a statement, as *Tete*Susan tried to help the two solve their marital problems.

"*Tete*, you have done a very good thing to come, because I was also planning to come to your house to have a chat with you. I am now being treated like a useless nobody in this house. I am seen as a brainless small child. If I talk to Netsai, she does not respond. If I reprimand the children, she teams with them against me. To tell you the truth, I am not happy in this house," Herbert said.

Netsai could not control her anger, "Herbert, you must learn to say the truth! Everything started with the money you took from the bank without telling me, and the money you collected from our lodgers, which you did not deposit into our account."

"*Tete*, do I have to tell my wife everything I plan to do with other men? As a businessman, there are other things I have to do with other men?"

"Businessman? Which businesses do you own, which I am not aware of?" Netsai was trying hard to maintain her composure.

"Oh! You thought you were the only one who can own businesses? You want to take me for a ride! There is nothing like that anymore." Herbert punctuated his anger by banging the coffee table with his fist.

"I want my money back here where it belongs...."

Before she could finish what she was saying, Herbert, who was visibly angry, stood up.

"You want to take me for a fool?" *Tete*Susan and her husband stood up to restrain Herbert if need be.

"Why can't you young people respect us? We came here to help you sort out your differences?" *Va*Simon said as he restrained Herbert.

"Netsai, please have respect for us," *Tete*Susan said, holding her protectively from Herbert. She took Netsai to her bedroom.

When the children heard the commotion, they woke up and began to cry. Netsai and *Tete*Susan took them back to their rooms. *Tete* begged Netsai to stop talking about the money, which Herbert had squandered since that was causing the tension in the house.

"Herbert, don't beat your wife each time you get angry. It is not good. What if she dies?" *Va*Simon was talking to Herbert, who did not respond.

"Anything that causes tension in your house, come and tell us, we will try to help you solve your differences," *Tete*Susan said, as she walked back into the lounge after leaving Netsai in her bedroom.

"That's alright, *Tete*. Forgive me for losing my temper in front of you. Netsai is not treating me like a man of the house these days," Herbert said, trying to make himself appear like a good husband.

"Live well with your wife, Herbert, not this cat and mouse business."

"We are not going to stay for much longer. We are going. Please stay well," *Tete*Susan said as she and her husband stood up to leave.

Herbert walked them to their car.

Netsai's aunt was worried about her niece because she realised that although she had tried to solve the problem, she could not get to the bottom of the matter. She realised that there was nothing much she could do to help Netsai, since her father was not willing to help his daughter.

That night Netsai and Herbert hardly slept because they were shouting at each other. In the morning Netsai went to Samuel, her brother's place. She explained everything to Samuel, who was not surprised at all by Herbert's behaviour, because he had seen him and Aida at several places in Harare. Most of the time he had seen them together, he had quickly left the place before Herbert saw him.

Samuel did not hide his anger towards Herbert. He rang him at work and gave him a piece of his mind. Samuel told Herbert that he would look after his sister well, instead of brutalising her like Herbert did. Netsai stayed with Samuel for over a month. Netsai and

Samuel's wife had a good relationship. They went to women's social associations together and other social gatherings. But there were two people who were not happy with Netsai staying at her brother's place. These were her parents. They wanted her to return to her husband, but Samuel was adamant that Netsai would live with him.

During the course of Netsai's absence, Herbert went to *Tete*Susan to request her help to bring Netsai back home, but Netsai refused. *Tete*Susan decided to bring the matter to Netsai's mother. Netsai's mother, who wanted Netsai to go back to her husband, decided to vent her anger at Samuel's wife, whom she accused of misleading Netsai. Netsai realised that her mother's behaviour could end up affecting her brother and his wife's relationship, so she decided to put the matter to rest and return to her home.

Immediately after two weeks, Herbert went back to his old self and began to sleep out again. Netsai realised that one cannot teach a bird to sing a new song, or teach an old dog new tricks. Herbert no longer beat Netsai because he did not want to leave her with any incriminating evidence to show her parents. He knew it was hard for Netsai to prove that Herbert was not spending most of his nights at home. Netsai also realised that she could not use the reason of her husband's not sleeping at home to convince her parents that her marriage should end. If they could not accept her when she was brutally beaten, she knew that they could not accept her for any other reason.

Meanwhile, Herbert and *Va*Mungofa, Aida's sister's husband, were making preparations to go and pay *lobola* for Aida.

CHAPTER Seven

Herbert arranged a delegation to go and pay *lobola* for Aida. The delegation comprised an intermediary - *munyai*, *Va*Mungofa and some friends that he had met through Aida. None of his family, apart from his mother, knew that he was going to pay lobola for Aida. They filled two cars with groceries, which ranged from meat, soap, cooking oil, sugar, powdered milk, salt, tea leaves, Vaseline and body lotion, toilet paper, rice, refined mealie-meal, sweets, fruits and drinks which included beer and soft drinks. He bought a whole pig and a whole goat for braai.

When they arrived at Aida's village, they parked their cars at Aida aunt's house, where they remained until the *lobola* procedure began. By customary rules, Herbert and his team were not allowed to come into direct contact with Aida's parents, or go into her parents' house before the formalities of the *lobola* payment were performed. Therefore, it was at Aida's aunt that the groceries were unloaded from the car and checked. Most of the female relatives in the village were assembled in that house.

Among the women relatives, was an old woman, almost in her seventies, who was in charge of the female group. She was the village elder, respected by all the women who had taken marriage counsel and guidance from her. She was full of humour and knew how to entertain people. Everyone in the village called her *Ambuya*.

"Can you show me what this man has brought for his in- laws, bring all the boxes here. I will open one by one and bring him to task if there is something missing. I will admonish him," *Ambuya* said and a young lad of about fifteen brought the boxes to the woman amidst laughter from the other women in the hut.

Ambuya emptied the contents of the boxes, checking every item and sometimes making jokes about things she did not know. Each time she was nodding her head in approval, until she fished out a small bottle of cooking oil. It was a 750ml bottle. She held it towards the intermediary.

"What do you call this? Umm? What is this?"

"It's cooking oil *Ambuya...*" but *Ambuya* interjected.

"So you think I am a village idiot who can not tell that it's cooking oil?" she said, grinning to expose wide gaps between her teeth. Every one in the room laughed.

"Today they will feel the wrath of *Ambuya*," a young woman whispered.

"You bring this tiny bottle of cooking oil; do you think we are a bunch of *hardies*? Were you buying it for your girlfriend?" Everyone broke into laughter. Since it was a Saturday and schools were closed, many children of school going age had come to the homestead. A few were gathered around Herbert's car, listening to cassettes playing on the car radio at low volume.

"*Ambuya*, I did not know that you can speak slang," one of the young man said.

"I want them to see that I am hard as well. I am wise and tough, and that when it comes to city ways, I am their match. Otherwise they come here thinking that we are a village of illiterates," *Ambuya* said, adding to the laughter in the hut.

"I am sorry, *Ambuya*. We overlooked that. It is just that in the shop where we bought the cooking oil, they had only small bottles. We were looking for gallons but...."

"So what? Nevertheless, was it not wise to buy several small bottles instead of bringing just one bottle? You think I do not know Mathematics? If you had bought six of these, they would have made a gallon. I am also educated you know!" There was more laughter. The intermediary took out his wallet and fished a wad of crisp Z$50 bills. He gave *Ambuya* Z$300, which was enough to buy five gallons of cooking oil.

"We are sorry, *Ambuya*, rest your case. Take this and buy more cooking oil," the *munyai* said as he handed *Ambuya* the money. She took it smiling, and tied it into the piece of cloth tied to her petticoat.

"Here, it's in a safe bank. No one will steal it," she said as she tied the knot.

Food was prepared shortly afterwards. The young women filled large teapots with milky tea, which they sweetened with loads of sugar before putting the teapots on glowing charcoal to keep warm. They sliced large slices of bread, and spread margarine and jam on them. They passed tea around. They filled a big teapot and put sliced bread on a big *rusero*, which they then took to the big house where the male relatives were sitting.

As soon as they finished drinking tea, the women cut chunky pieces of meat, which they began to cook, and also some rice and *sadza*. Outside, young boys had made a fire where they were roasting pork ribs and goat meat. The whole village was in a celebratory mood, much to Herbert's pleasure and satisfaction. He was feeling very important.

When everyone had had enough food, the ceremony for paying *lobola* began. Aida's uncle was responsible for charging the money. The intermediary was sitting on the floor, with his bag of money next to him. A big wooden plate was placed on a reed-mat where the intermediary would put whatever amount of money was asked for by the uncle. There was so much silence in the room, that one could hear the sound of rats running from one room to another or climbing the wall. Aida's uncle cleared his throat.

"I want to know who told you that I have a very beautiful daughter called Aida. Can you pay Z$100 for that, before we continue?"

The intermediary placed Z$100 in the plate. It was for *makandinzwa nani,* the money that every intermediary is asked to pay in any lobola ceremony.

"You all know that to raise a child is not easy. Your wife was playing with my beard when she was a toddler, sometimes pulling out my beard in the process. I want money for *matekenya ndebvu dzababa*-Z$100," the intermediary put the amount in the plate.

"And also your wife-to-be spent nine months in my wife's womb, kicking her womb, I want money for *mapfukudza dumbu* now, and that one make it Z$200," the intermediary put the money on the plate.

"And you also know that for your-wife-to-be, to grow up into the attractive and respectable woman she is, it took her aunts and elder sisters a lot of effort to groom her into a fine woman. Can you pay the aunts and sisters their dews, please?" I won't state the amount, the eldest aunt is here to speak for herself," the uncle said. The women whispered and agreed on a figure, which the intermediary paid.

When Aida's sisters asked for their pick, they demanded Z$3000.

"You girls, you surprise me. Instead of supporting us, you are taking all the money from us, and how are you going to start the new home with Herbert after you take all the money?" the middleman asked Aida's sisters after he realised that they were also being greedy.

"Don't worry about us, *Va*Makoni, when you run out of cash, there is an automated cash machine at the shops," one of the sisters said and the others giggled.

"And if the money in the ATM is finished? Where do we get more?" the intermediary asked, reproaching Aida's aunt and her sisters. "You will eat sadza and lacto in your new home," he added.

"What is an ATM?" one family friend asked.

"It's a bank machine which does not close. It operates 24/7" Biserck chipped in.

"Biserck, what is 24/7? You think we know arithmetic like you do?" the friend asked, showing confusion. The young people in the house laughed, including Aida.

"24/7 means that every day, every week. A day has twenty-four hours, and seven is for the number of days in a week," Biserck explained, feeling very important now.

"So we can say 24/7/365, can't we?" another young lad who wanted to show everyone that he knew his maths very well said, "365 for the number of days in a year....."

"Or 24/7/366 for a leap-year," another one said.

"You young people shut up! You want to show off with your education? We also went to school and we learnt to write on the scroll boards," *Ambuya* said "Or in the sand. We were writing our ABC and times table on the sand...."

Aida's uncle who had waited for everyone to keep quiet continued with the proceedings.

"Now we come to the main part, you know, to raise a child is very expensive these days, especially a girl child. If our daughter was not educated, you would not have come to ask for her hand-in-marriage. Can we have Z$5000 for that, please?"

Some people in the room registered shock on their faces, because Z$5000 was a lot, enough to pay a deposit for a house, but the intermediary put the required amount on the plate. Soon the plate was spilling with money. One of Aida's younger uncles took the plate to Aida's father, who emptied the contents into his briefcase. They would count it later and give some of it to his brothers.

The process went on and on, with money for this, and money for that being charged, and the intermediary paid almost everything. He was asked to pay the monetary value of ten cows and two goats, of which he paid. He was asked to pay money for Aida's parent's clothes. Aida's father said he wanted a double-breasted suit with a matching shirt, necktie, shoes, socks, walking stick, a leather briefcase, a wristwatch, a fashionable hat and a cardigan. Aida's mother said she wanted a two-piece georgette suit, a matching jacket, a handbag, wristwatch, shoes, socks, a wrapper and perfume. The intermediary paid Z$5000 for each parent's clothes. The wrapper was given to her straight away, because it was the custom that the new son-in-law gives it to the mother-in-law on the day he pays *lobola*. He also paid the monetary value for the mother's cow, which many people usually pay many years after the initial ceremony, but the intermediary wanted to prove to them that he was loaded.

Everyone was satisfied with the proceedings. There were smiles everywhere and people were drinking beer and cold drinks. The uncle who was responsible for charging the *lobola* was soon drunk. He could hardly stand, and was soon snoring. He had to be taken into one of the bedrooms to sleep while another uncle took over.

If the intermediary thought he had finished paying *lobola*, he was in for a shock. *Ambuya* was well known for asking for money known as *mari yembariro*, money for the *rafters*. When she cleared her throat for attention, people began to nudge each other. They knew what was coming.

"These men are very selfish. They charged all that belongs to the male department, but we never heard them charging money for the rafters." Women chuckled while Aida's mother could not hide her embarrassment "Yes, money for the rafters in that plate."

The intermediary did not know what money for the rafters meant because it was the first time he heard about it. He asked for explanation, much to the embarrassment of many in the room.

"You don't know money for the rafters? Where do you come from? Because where I was married it is charged, and you know I have been encouraging this area to emulate that practice. For Aida to be there," she said pointing at Aida, "her mother conceived her while she was lying with her back on the floor, facing the rafters. You women look at me as if I am a joke, isn't it time we take over this business of charging *lobola* from the males?" she chuckled and licked her lips. She was now drunk from the cold beer provided by Herbert. "Yes, women have to lie facing the rafters to conceive, and they face the rafters again to have babies, so you see, we want money for the roof. Aida's mother here did not face the rafters for men to benefit from this whole thing," she did not mince her words. She liked vulgar and obscene language, especially after drowning a few beers.

In the house, a *sahwira* called Biserck decided to explain further. "When you make a baby, the mother looks at the roof," he said in broken Shona language. He was originally from Malawi, and he was one of the Malawi immigrants who had come to Rhodesia to work in farms and mines. Villagers enjoyed it his accent and broken Shona language and they saw him as the village comedian.

"This thing about money for the rafters is something else. What happens when the child is conceived in the bush, when there is no roof or ceiling?" someone asked.

"Ah, she will charge money for the sky in that case," Biserck replied and there was more laughter. The intermediary just shook his head in amusement. He knew there were some families who were really greedy when they married their daughters, and this family was the worst he had ever come across. The *munyai* was asked to pay Z$500.00 for the rafters, and he grudgingly paid it.

"Ah, this *mukwasha* is *lich* (rich). After paying all this money, everything in full and no balance, you must give him two wives," said Biserck and everyone laughed. People were now enjoying themselves and cracking jokes while drinking beer and having braai meat.

"No, I am not joking. This man has money, if you don't give him two wives he will go and pay *lobola* for one or two more wives. I am serious," there was more laughter. By the end of the ceremony, the whole village was happy and satisfied.

After paying money for *kupinda mumusha* for the new son-in-law to come and greet his in-laws, Herbert was escorted into the room by *Va*Mungofa, Aida's brother-in-law. The formalities of introducing Herbert to the family were carried out and the house broke into a party. Herbert had proved to them that he had money. Aida was now married to a very rich man from Harare, the news spread throughout the village.

After the ceremony, Aida and Herbert got into their car and drove off.

"Where are we going, Herbert?" Aida asked after she saw Herbert take a different route from the one going towards Harare.

"It's a surprise. Close your eyes and open them when we get to our destination," Herbert enjoyed pleasing Aida with his numerous surprises.

They arrived at Nyanga Hotel before sunset. Aida was surprised and excited at the same time. She hugged Herbert and kissed him. They spent the rest of the weekend at the hotel. On Monday, Herbert phoned in sick and spent two more days at the hotel, enjoying himself, swimming in the big pools, playing games and walking around Inyanga Mountain. When the honeymoon was over, Herbert took Aida to her sister's place, where she continued to live with *Va*Mungofa and his wife, much to Aida's disappointment as she wanted her own place with Herbert, but there she was, continuing to live in her sister's house.

CHAPTER Eight

One day Herbert came from work and found Aida very moody and refusing to talk to him. She even refused to eat food while Herbert was there. Herbert thought that it was because Aida was now pregnant.

"Shake hands, young man. Is it true that you are expecting twins?" *Va*Mungofa asked Herbert, who just nodded, grinning. "You fired *doubles* isn't it? You are a real man."

"Stop it, men will never grow up!" Aida's sister said.

"What? I want to attend the baby shower, I will dress like a woman in a wig," *Va*Mungofa teased his wife. He also wanted to cheer up Aida who was visibly cross.

"We will invite you. There are many wigs in this house," Aida's sister joked. "You hear what your mate here is planning, *Babamudiki?*" she was now addressing Herbert. Herbert just laughed. Aida was now six months pregnant, but since it was her first pregnancy, it was not showing yet.

Herbert followed Aida to the bedroom to find out what the problem was, but when Herbert got into the bedroom, Aida began to read a book.

"What's the matter, Aida?"

"Nothing, just leave me alone, I want to sleep," she replied, burying her head in the book.

"If there is something bothering you, say it, Aida," Herbert said.

"For how long are we going to be staying here with my sister's family? You have three houses, yet I still live with my sister. Very soon I will be having two babies, can't you see there is not enough space here?"

"Can you bear it a few more weeks? I need to give the tenants in Glen View notice to leave the house."

"Herbert, you think I am the type that would want to live in high density areas?" Aida felt offended by Herbert's proposal.

"Umm, I can see that today you are really in a bad mood. I will evict the tenant in Milton Park, then. I will give them a short notice to vacate my house," Herbert said trying to reach out to Aida, who smiled. That week he went to Milton Park where he told the tenant to find alternative accommodation because in two week's time he wanted to use the house for something else. The tenant tried to negotiate with him, but to no avail.

"Couldn't you allow us to serve the recommended three month's notice?" *Amai*Mandy asked.

"I can't do that because I need to use the house for something else as soon as possible," he replied.

"What about school children? We can't just move out like that. We need to transfer the children to new schools, so couldn't you just let them finish the term?"

"If it's so hard, then you can move into the two small rooms at the back, the *boys kaya*...."

"What about all our property, *Va*Kudzingwa? We have property filling four bedrooms, the lounge and dining rooms. Where do we put all that when we move into those two tiny rooms?" *Mai*Mandy couldn't believe what Herbert was proposing.

"I can put your furniture in the garage."

*Amai*Mandy saw that Herbert was determined, and knew that she had to look for a new place to rent the following morning.

Herbert went and told Aida that they would be moving to Milton Park in two weeks. Aida was very pleased. She couldn't wait to start measuring the curtains and looking for new furniture.

Unbeknown to Netsai, she went to Milton Park the following week to collect money from *Amai*Mandy for the following month's rent.

"We can't pay money to you for next month. Actually, we want the money we paid for deposit when we moved in. You did not give us enough notice."

Netsai looked expressionless. She did not know what AmaiMandy was on about.

"You look surprised. Don't you know what is happening?" AmaiMandy asked.

"To be honest with you, no, I don't know what you are on about," Netsai said.

"Your husband gave us only two weeks notice to leave, and we were very lucky to find another house in the area, so we are actually in the process of packing our things to move out," AmaiMandy explained.

"I knew nothing about this, AmaiMandy. I am very sorry, truly sorry. My husband doesn't explain things to me anymore," Netsai was on the verge of tears.

"It's unbelievable, AmaiFarai. I used to think that people with loads of money are very happy, but I was wrong," AmaiMandy said, feeling sorry for Netsai. "I used to admire your family, but now it's different," AmaiMandy had seen Aida coming to inspect the house and take measurements for the curtains. She had also noticed that Aida was pregnant, but did not tell Netsai any of that.

"It's hard, AmaiMandy. I have to go," Netsai said. She bade AmaiMandy farewell and left feeling humiliated, but before she left, AmaiMandy gave her the address of where she was going to live.

Netsai was considering going to Herbert's work place to ask him what it was he wanted to use the house for because Herbert had not been to Eastlea for quite a long time. She also wanted to get her car from Herbert, so that she could use it for her deliveries. She was feeling sorry for herself, despite all the hard work, she was presently living in misery. She pondered on AmaiMandy's words and saw the truth in them. Before they had a lot of money, her family was a happy one. Money and wealth seemed to have brought a curse in her life. She went to a small shop where she bought herself a drink, but did not finish the drink because she was feeling depressed. She gave it to a *street kid* who could not believe his luck. She decided to go home.

* * *

Meanwhile Herbert and Aida were buying new furniture in the best furniture shops in the city.

"What time can you deliver the furniture?" Aida asked the shopkeeper.

Tomorrow, mid-morning."

"Can't you do it late afternoon, because I need to clean the place in the morning?" Aida asked the sales representatives.

"Yes, I think the afternoon is better," Herbert supported Aida's proposal.

"No problem. We do what the customer wants because in our shop, the customer is the king," the customer representative said.

"Thank you, sir. We will see you tomorrow when you bring the furniture," Herbert said as he left the shop arm-in arm with Aida.

* * *

When Netsai arrived home, she just went to bed straight, fully clothed, in spite of the hot tropical heat that afternoon. She was sweating and palpitating, but despite that, she pulled the quilt over her head.

When Farai came from school, he found his mother sleeping, with a quilt over her.

"Mum, what is it? Is it still about dad? Where is he staying?"

"I don't know, my son, I am at a loss for words."

"Have you tried to find out where he is?"

"Who can tell me, my son?" she asked.

"I think you should go to his work place to check," Farai was really worried about his mother.

"Don't worry, Farai, when he is ready, he will come back."

Farai remained quiet, looking at his mother as if he wanted to say something, but deciding against it. Netsai stared at her son's school blazer, which was faded. She looked at his shoes. They were in a very bad shape. The shoes had holes and the soles were nearly gone. When Farai walked, he walked like a person with some rickets because of his shoes. Farai noticed what his mother was staring at him and his eyes welled with tears.

"I will buy another blazer and a new pair of shoes, Farai, if I raise enough money from my sewing business. Things will be alright eventually, Farai. God is for everyone." Farai nodded.

"Mum, I also think it is important for me to drop out of the basketball team. I don't have proper trainers, so if I stop playing the sport, we can save the money," Farai said.

"I don't want you to quit your favourite sport, Farai. I will see what we can do. Basketball is your talent. I will help you realize your goal."

"I told my teacher today that I am intending to quit the sport, and he suggested that I may be able to get a scholarship. He said he will apply for one on my behalf," Farai told his mother.

"Then I think we should wait to see how that comes out, before you leave the sport. I just hope you will get the scholarship my son," Netsai's eyes were welling up, but she did her best to control her emotions.

"The reason I am deciding to quit the sport is because if my application for the scholarships is turned down, I will be hurt and it will affect me, mama, so it's better I just stop playing the game," Farai said.

"You will get it, Farai. You are very talented and besides, God does not give one person more burdens than he or she can bear. Something will work out for you. We need to have faith. I will pray hard for your dream to come true."

CHAPTER Nine

Aida was making preparations to move into her new house. She woke up very early and went to Milton Park. She began to clean the house and hang her photographs in the lounge and dining rooms. When the furniture was delivered in the afternoon, the place was immaculately clean. She instructed the deliverymen to put the furniture where she wanted it to be, and very soon, the house was full of brand new furniture. She threw herself on one of the sofas, patted her stomach and fell asleep, only to be woken up by Herbert's kiss on the cheek. They went to a hotel to eat, celebrating their new home together.

* * *

Netsai was desperate to find out who had moved into their Milton Park house, so she left early to go to Milton Park. She saw her car, the one that Herbert was using, parked in the driveway. She knocked on the door, her heart beating very fast. A female voice responded, asking her to come in to the house.

She was greeted by a photograph of Aida and Herbert, which was displayed in the lounge. Aida came to check who their visitor was, and when she saw Netsai, she retreated into the passage and went to the bedroom to call Herbert.

"What do you want here?" Herbert asked, covering his groin with a dressing gown. He was angry.

"*Babava*Farai, what is this you are doing?"

"I don't want to see you here again. I bought you a house in Eastlea, that's where you must stay, not here. This is my house with Aida. In fact, this is now Aida's house, do you hear me?"

"*Babava*Farai, you did not buy me a house. We bought these houses together. It's my house and my children's house. If you want a house for Aida then you...."

"Don't make me lose my temper now, because I will soon teach you a lesson," Herbert said, moving towards Netsai. Aida was standing behind Herbert watching what was happening.

"You are a shameless beast!" Netsai reached for the portraits on the wall and began to smash them on the floor. She reached for the television set and threw it down, smashing the screen. Herbert tried to restrain her, but she was very angry. She reached for the flower vase, which had neatly arranged flowers and threw it at Aida. Aida ran into the bedroom where she locked herself in. Herbert managed to push Netsai out of the house.

"Give me the car keys. I need my car!" Netsai screamed

"Which car? Do you have a car?" Herbert said as he shoved Netsai outside.

"You are a shameless man! How can you abandon your family to live with a whore?"

"You are the whore because you don't have a husband anymore! It's over between us. Aida is now my wife, Mrs Kudzingwa for your own information!" Herbert was very angry and wanted to beat Netsai.

Netsai saw danger looming and fled.

"So, I work and another woman just comes to enjoy the fruits of my sweat?" She shouted from the gate.

"Leave Aida alone and f—k off!" Aida was watching everything through the window.

"We will meet again Herbert. It's not over!" Netsai shouted back.

"We will meet where? Bitch!"

* * *

Netsai went to Mufakose to inform her aunt of the new developments.

"I never thought it would come to this. When he takes your house and give it to another woman, I think you need to tell his relatives," *Tete*Susan suggested.

"You think they don't know?"

"Yes, it's possible."

"Aunty, it is not easy for someone to go and pay *lobola* for a new wife without the family's blessings," Netsai said.

"Such things happen, Netsai. Ask me, I have seen a lot with my eyes. Maybe they are as ignorant as we were all," *Tete*Susan said. "When a man starts behaving like Herbert, and has numerous lovers, it's most likely that he does his things with his friends."

"I will go to his brother this evening to let him know what is happening. I don't really know who to trust anymore, but I feel so hurt, aunty."

Netsai went to Herbert's brother, Lameck's house, that same evening, where she found *Amai*Rujeko, Lameck's wife, sitting on the veranda.

"Welcome *Amai*Farai," *Amai*Rujeko said, embracing Netsai. "These days you are scarce *Amainini*, you must be very busy?"

"Too many things to do, *Amai*Rujeko," Netsai said, making herself comfortable on the mat where her sister-in-law was also sitting. "How is the family, *Amaiguru*?"

"They are well. How is yours? I think Farai is now a very big man."

Netsai kept quiet for a while as if she had gone into another world. Netsai's sister-in-law, *Amai*Rujeko, could see that there was something troubling Netsai and that her thoughts were somewhere else. She decided to find out what it was that was troubling her sister-in-law.

"Are you okay *Amainini*."

"Things are not well for me *Amaiguru*."

"What is the problem?"

"Ah, *Amaiguru*, my house is on fire. I am really troubled, that is why I came here to see you and your husband," Netsai said.

"What is it, *Amai*Farai? When you and your husband are quiet and don't come to see us, we just assume that all is well. What is it?" She was showing genuine concern.

"*Amaiguru*, your *Babamudiki* does not live at home anymore. He is now living in Milton Park with a new wife."

"What do you mean a new wife, *Amai*Farai?" *Amai*Rujeko moved closer to Netsai and hugged her. "What do you mean he is living with another wife? What has really gone into Herbert's head?"

"This is what has happened to me, my *sister*," Netsai's eyes welled and warm tears rolled down her cheeks. She used the back of her hand to try and stop the tears, but to no avail.

"I can't believe this...." Her husband's car pulled up at the gate before she finished what she wanted to say. "Your brother-in-law is here now. You can tell him what is happening."

"That's better because I was really worried that I would leave very late if he had not come home early," Netsai said, pulling herself together.

"Are you not driving?" *Amai*Rujeko asked, because she thought Netsai had parked her car outside the gate.

"Driving? Those are now by-gones. Herbert took my car. That's the one he is using with his new wife," Netsai replied.

"It's sad, my *sister*. That's why they say the right hand ploughs and does all the work, for the left hand to eat. How can Herbert make you slave for another woman?"

Herbert's brother entered the house. Netsai and *Amai*Rujeko had moved into the house when it was becoming a bit chilly on the veranda.

"It's going to rain today. *Amai*Farai is in my home. This is surely a surprise!" Lameck said, giving Netsai a handshake. "It's not good to be so scarce *Amainini*." They exchanged the customary greetings, both clapping their hands.

"How are you *Mufakose*?" Netsai asked, using Herbert's family totem.

"I am well, *Amainini*. How are the children, and Farai who no longer comes to see us? Did you instruct him not to come to see us?" he asked jokingly.

"No, *Babamukuru*, it's just that we can be very busy and keep procrastinating," she replied.

"I am going to hang my jacket and neck-tie in the wardrobe, *Mai*Farai, I will be with you in a minute," Lameck said, going into the bedroom. "It's a bit warm today."

*Amai*Rujeko pretended to go to the kitchen to get some drinks, but followed her husband in the bedroom, where she spoke to him in a hushed tone. "*Baba*vaRujeko, that story you told me about Herbert marrying a second wife is true! That's why *Amai*Farai is here," she said.

"This man is bringing himself down. I don't know what has gone into his head," Lameck said, shaking his head. "Is it money which is making him lose his head?"

"Let me go back into the lounge," *Amai*Rujeko said. She went to the kitchen first where she prepared some cold drinks and put them on a tray, together with a small plate of biscuits.

"I thought I might get carried away with chatting and forget to offer you a drink," *Amai*Rujeko said to Netsai, as she placed the drinks on the table.

"You shouldn't have bothered yourself, *Amaiguru*," Netsai said.

"No, it's not a bother. I also wanted something to drink," *Amai*Rujeko said. She began to pour some drinks into glasses and put biscuits in the plates. She gave Netsai a glass of fanta. Just then, Lameck walked into the lounge fully changed from his work clothes.

"How is your sewing business going, *Amai*Farai?" he asked.

"It's not so bad," Netsai replied. She did not look at her brother-in-law in the eyes.

"You don't sound certain whether the business is doing good or not, what's the matter?" he asked again because he could see that Netsai was dodging his gaze.

"That is one of the reasons I am here, *Babamukuru*," Netsai said. "Since *Babava*Farai started to take money from the shop, the business isn't performing very well. It has gone down."

"Is he taking money from the shop? Shameless man! We all know that you are the proprietor of the sewing shop, why is he doing that? He doesn't seem to realize that he is committing a serious customary offence."

"That's not all, *Babamukuru*. Now he is living with another woman in our house in Milton Park. He started by collecting money from the tenants and not paying it back, then he went on to take money from the transport business, with no explanation at all as to how he was using the money."

"How long has he been doing that?"

"It's now more than a year, I think the woman is actually pregnant. I saw her today."

"Why didn't you come to tell me, *Amai*Farai? You shouldn't have allowed it to happen for this long without telling me." Lameck was genuinely worried.

"I thought he would soon get over it and get back to his usual self."

"You were right my *sister.* Our elders have a saying that the roof conceals a lot. You can't just go about telling everyone your business," *Amai*Rujeko said.

"There are things you can conceal, but you can not conceal something with horns because the horns will grow big and cut through the cover. One thumb cannot squeeze a louse. Some issues need combined effort to tackle." Lameck said. "If you keep a burden like this to yourself you can suffer from high blood pressure. As your husband's brother, you were supposed to come and inform me about all these things. How can you keep such things to yourself for over a year?"

"I made a mistake, *Babamukuru*, I am sorry," Netsai replied.

"*Babava*Rujeko is right. We hear of people who just collapse and die from stress-related illnesses all because they were burdened with problems they didn't share and get solved," *Amai*Rujeko said.

"I will go to his workplace tomorrow and find out from him what he is really up to. I will try my best to resolve this."

"Thank you, *Babamukuru* and *Amaiguru*. I am not staying much longer. I have to go before it gets dark," Netsai said, clapping her hands.

"Let me drive you to the bus stop. I am going to get the keys for my car," Lameck said as he went into the bedroom to fetch the car keys.

"My sister, just keep your mouth shut, don't provoke him," *Amai*Rujeko advised.

"It's very annoying, *Amaiguru*, and also heartbreaking, but I will try my best to do as you say," Netsai promised.

"People change. I would never have thought Herbert would behave like this; such a quiet person?" *Amai*Rujeko sighed. "I am really at a loss for words," she clasped her hands together.

"It happens in life," Netsai said as she stood up to leave. "I will see you soon," she said. Her in-laws took her to the local bus stop and left after she got a bus.

* * *

When Netsai arrived home, she was greeted by Farai who gave her a letter from his school. She opened it and was excited by the news.

Divorce Token

Dear Mr and Mrs Kudzingwa

We have are pleased to inform you that your son has been awarded a Basketball Scholarship by Kubhururuka Corporations to study for the next four years at this school. He will be provided with uniforms and pocket money. He will also receive a full sports kit. This scholarship also includes boarding fees.

We wish you all the best.

Yours sincerely

Mr N. Kugara

The Headmaster

Netsai broke into a cry of joy. "The Lord heard my prayers," she said. She was very excited. She hugged Farai as tears of joy poured down her cheeks. "I didn't know what to do about your fees, but now there is nothing to stop you from finishing your studies, Farai."

"Mama, I am going to continue with my education up to university level. I was intending to leave school after my GCSEs to save you money, but now the money issue is solved. I just need to work hard. Mama, the headmaster also said he got me a holiday job. He wants to know if you approve."

"I wouldn't say no to anything like that my son. How can I refuse opportunities for you?" Netsai was all smiles. "God answered my prayers. Now I have to deal with Tariro alone."

After supper, Farai did his homework. There was happiness again in that house, and Netsai felt she had learnt a lesson of life that day. There is always light after darkness.

The following morning she went to see *Tete*Susan to discuss her meeting with Lameck and his wife.

"You know what my niece, now that there are two of you married to your husband, you need to be very strong."

"How do I do that?" Netsai asked, puzzled.

"We need to go and see a traditional healer, a *n'anga*, who can give you some concoctions to cleanse you," *Tete*Susan said. "I suggest we go there now if you have time."

"I don't see how that can help me, *Tete*. The other time you gave me some concoctions Herbert only stayed home for a week. It even became worse because he went on to marry another woman? I don't trust these things, *Tete*."

"You keep topping up the *muti*, my dear. You will top up the one I gave you with the one we will get from the traditional-healer that we are going to see. If you are not careful, Herbert will leave you for good."

Netsai did not hide her unwillingness to go to see the female *n'anga* (traditional healer). Her aunt left her in the house and went to consult the woman. She was given a bundle of concoctions, with instructions on how to use them.

Unbeknown to *Tete*Susan, Aida was also consulting the same *n'anga* for love potions and concoctions to keep Herbert to herself. Just as *Tete* Susan left the traditional healer's house, Aida arrived at the healer's house to seek for the same concoctions to keep Herbert under her skirt.

"That car looks like *Amai*Farai's. I am sure it's her car," *Tete*Susan said to herself when she saw the car Herbert was using now parked near the traditional healer's house. "I told Netsai that Aida is not taking things for granted. I am sure she has also come to look for the same concoctions. Or may be it's not Netsai's car, but I doubt it," she said as she walked away. "It was a good thing that Netsai did not come with me; otherwise things would have gone the other way. Imagine two adversaries coming face to face at a place like this," she said.

She arrived home and explained to Netsai how she was supposed to use the use the *muti.*

"You use this one for bathing, and this one, you cook and mix with porridge...." *Tete*Susan explained, but Netsai was not interested. She accepted the concoctions dutifully.

In the traditional healer's house, Aida was given the same mix of concoctions. When she arrived home, she put her concoctions in a secure place and began to prepare supper. She mixed the relish with one of the concoctions. She went to the bathroom, filled the tub with warm water and sprinkled some of the concoctions and soaked herself. As usual, Herbert was fed Aida's food, which was cooked and mixed with concoctions from traditional healers from all over the country, unbeknown to him.

"This is delicious," Herbert said as he ate the food. "I like your cooking. It's always safer to eat food from your own house these days. If I eat your *sadza* every lunch hour I will grow really big and healthy," he said, rolling morsels of *sadza* and chewing joyously.

"As long as I am on maternity leave, I can cook *sadza* for your lunch and you can come home to eat," Aida replied, glad that her concoctions were effective. Herbert kissed Aida on the cheek when he had finished eating, before he returned to work.

CHAPTER Ten

Hebert was at work when his elder brother phoned him. He addressed his elder brother, *Baba*Rujeko, as *mudhara* - old man.

"How are you, *mudhara*?" He asked.

"I am well. How is work?"

"Why do you talk as if you are unwell, *mudhara*?" Herbert asked because his brother's voice was barely audible; it sounded as if he had flu.

"Ah! I think maybe it's a hangover."

"Only that! Just tell me if you want me to buy you more beer, which can cure a hangover." Herbert tried to cheer his brother up.

"Yes, that's the parable talk of elders when they want something," *Babava*Rujeko replied.

"Can we meet in the Jo'berg lines soon after work," Herbert suggested. Jo'berg Lines were popularly known as Majubheki; a section of Mbare Township named after the famous Johannesburg city of South Africa.

After work Herbert drove straight to Jo'berg Lines, and went to *Va*Mujubhegi, also named after the sprawling suburb, who ran a prominent shebeen in the area, where she sold unlicensed liquor in her private house. Herbert's brother arrived soon after and the two were drinking pint after pint and having braai meat. They went to sit in Herbert's brother's car, because *Babava*Rujeko had indicated that he needed some privacy, somewhere they could talk family business without the fear of being overheard. Herbert knew that his brother would not just call him to drink beer only, unless there was family business to discuss. *Babava*Rujeko started by talking about other things, meandering until he got to the heart of the matter.

"Herbert, *Amai*Farai came to my house with disturbing news. What is really happening?" Herbert knew exactly that the visit was special otherwise his brother would not have met with him simply to tell him that his wife had visited them. Herbert just grinned. He did not respond.

"She told me that you no longer sleep in your house. Is it true?"

"Ah, *mudhara*, why do you listen to women so much?" Herbert's reply lacked the concern and seriousness that the subject under discussion deserved.

"Please, this is not a joke, *Munin'ina*. Let's treat this discussion with utmost seriousness," Lameck said, not hiding his fury at Herbert's lack of concern.

"*Mudhara....*" Herbert seemed taken aback and did not know how to respond.

"Is it true, my brother, that you are now living with another woman?" the voice was furious.

"Aa-a ya," Herbert was fidgeting with his car keys.

"Herbert, how can you live with a woman who is not known by any of your relatives? If something happens tomorrow, how are you going to approach us for help?" Lameck was displeased with his young brother's behaviour, because even though Herbert did not deny it or accept the allegation, his attitude said it all.

"I know what I am doing brother," Herbert replied, feigning anger at his brother's reproach. "The problem with you *mudhara* is that you still see me as a child. I am a grown up man for goodness sake," Herbert was getting out of his brother's car in protest. In truth, he was behaving like a cornered wounded tiger, hiding in his own anger and not wanting to admit his wrongs, not even to his own brother. Lameck was dumbfounded.

"Herbert, am I no longer your brother, the one who guides you when you go astray?"

"Brother, or no brother, please treat me as an adult. A married man with his own family and not a little boy!"

Herbert was now walking towards his car. Lameck got out of his car and followed him, still trying to reach out to Herbert and get to the bottom of what was really happening in his life. As an elder brother, he did not only have to assume a fatherly role for his young brother, but since Netsai had come to him, Shona custom demanded that he help restore peace in his brother's house.

"Herbert, a man who has an extended family to rely on, someone who has been brought and raised under strict Shona customs does not behave like that. You do not do your own things if you have a family. You let others know what is happening; otherwise this habit of secrets will backfire! Listen to me. I am your brother."

Herbert pretended as if he had heard nothing, or was not hearing anything at all. He was as stubborn and arrogant as ever. He got into his car, closed his door and started his engine. Within a few minutes, his car had left a cloud of dust and smoke in Lameck's face, who looked on in disbelief, mouth wide open until he choked and coughed. He had inhaled dust left behind by Herbert's car. Lameck walked back to his car and saw that there was a small crowd of spectators watching the free entertainment he and his brother had been putting up. He had forgotten that in Mbare, like in any other high-density places, incidents like this one attracted attention.

CHAPTER Eleven

Herbert was fuming. "This woman has outgrown her shoes. I am going to teach her a lesson. Bad mouthing me like that to every Jack-and-Jill...." Herbert was talking through clenched teeth. Anyone seeing the way the car was speeding would have easily mistaken it for a police car pursuing hijackers. He did not care about the speed limit and humps that were on the streets of Mbare. Vendors, beggars, small children and drunkards returning from their daily activities scurried away from the road, running for dear life.

When he arrived home, his children did not know how to react, whether to run and give him a hug, or hide in their rooms. They kept their distance from their visibly angry father. Herbert pushed past them, forcing them to one side of the passage hall and nearly knocked the youngest one over. He went straight to the main bedroom.

Unaware of Herbert's early home-coming, Netsai had been busy looking at the love concoctions, which she had left spread on the bed when she went to the bathroom.

"*Amai*Farai!" Herbert shouted when he saw the concoctions on the bed. Netsai came out of the bathroom and ran into the bedroom, hoping to hide the concoctions before Herbert saw them, but she was too late. In the bathroom she was about to prepare the bathing concoction but got disturbed by Herbert's unannounced visit.

"What is the matter, Herbert?" Netsai asked as she ran her eyes on the bed. She nearly fainted with embarrassment. Herbert was holding the concoctions in his hands.

"Herbert, Herbert! Am I your boyfriend? You must answer me with respect. You need to go back to your aunt for lessons on how to respect a husband! And now, what is this?" Herbert was examining the concoctions. The colour on Netsai's face drained, leaving her looking greyish like someone who had just seen a ghost. She was tongue-tied. Realising that Herbert was becoming angry and could be violent she decided to leave the bedroom, but Herbert followed her to the lounge.

"If your witch-doctors advised you to kill me so that you can inherit my wealth, my houses, then they got it all wrong," Herbert walked out of the bedroom, still clutching the concoctions in his hand. "It is over between us! I am divorcing you right here, right now, you crazy witch!" Herbert fished out a Z$2 note and threw it at Netsai. "You know what this is? *Igupuro,* a divorce token, to show your parents that we are no longer married. Foolish woman! Out of my house now!" Herbert barked.

Netsai picked the Z$2 note and quickly walked out of the house without looking back. She was very terrified of Herbert. "You go around saying bad things about me to my relatives! Idiot!" Herbert was shouting after Netsai, who was now opening the gate. She was soon swallowed by the dark night and did not hear some of the things Herbert was saying. Her children just stood by, watching their mother leave.

When she was a few yards away from the house, and certain that Herbert was not following her, Netsai rested her back against a dimly lit tower light.

"I must be dreaming. Is it real or am I imagining things? Life can easily change and put you on the receiving end. Is this the Herbert I married, a man who always listened to my opinion before we made any decisions? God, why have you forsaken me like this?" she said aloud, looking at the sky as if hoping to see God and get answers. She resumed walking on the dimly lit street. As she got further away from the house, she became scared of thieves. Her mind was now on a roller-costar, thinking about this and that, and also talking aloud. Anyone seeing her in that condition would have concluded that she was insane. But as afraid as she was of the night, she continued to walk and took a turn towards the main road, Enterprise Road, into the city centre.

Apart from the Z$2, which she had been given as a divorce token, she had no other money on her, making it impossible to hitch-hike to Mufakose where her parents lived. She walked until she became tired, but she had no choice but to keep on walking because she did not want to get to Mufakose in the middle of the night when robbers and thieves would prey on her. She decided to take a short break at a market stall specializing in selling handcrafts.

The young man who guarded the stall at night was surprised to see a woman asking for a place to rest at that time of the night. He offered her a stool to sit on, and asked her what had happened to her, forcing her to walk at night.

"My *sister*, why are you walking at this time of the night? Are you aware of the dangers you are putting yourself into because these roads in Eastlea are havens of thieves? Whatever it is that brought you out tonight, couldn't it have waited till tomorrow so that you could walk in daylight?" But Netsai did not reply the inquisitive young man. She just asked for water to drink.

"Can you give me some water to drink, my *brother*; my chest is burning with thirst?" She managed to say as she sat on the stool.

The young man ran to the nearby Service Station to get water and brought water in a small container, which he handed to Netsai. Netsai, who was too thirsty and too confused to notice a small mug near where she was sitting, drank the water straight from the container. The young man just watched her, before offering Netsai a place to sleep at that market stall.

"*Sister*, I advise you to make yourself comfortable here and proceed with your journey in the morning, otherwise you may never reach where you are going because of thieves and night killers," he advised. Netsai just shook her head, and did not say anything.

"You will be attacked by thieves or rapists or whatever danger is lurking in the darkness out there. Ahead, there is a very dark spot where thieves lurk," he said, pointing towards the road leading to the city centre." If you stay here, there are many people around so you will be protected. There are security guards manning the Service Station, and other night watchmen guarding those shops over there, so you will be safe here," he suggested, worried about how vulnerable Netsai was.

"Can you not walk with me, *brother*, until we walk past the dark spot you mentioned?" Netsai suggested, fear registered in her eyes. "When I get into the city centre I will see what I can do," she said.

"If I leave these crafts unmanned, my job will be finished, I will be fired tomorrow. Just make yourself at home," the young man insisted. But Netsai shook her head in refusal.

"Why can't you hitch-hike? There is still transport going towards the city," the man asked. Netsai laughed; an empty laughter filled with sorrow.

"I don't have any money to pay for a lift," Netsai replied, showing the young man the Z$2 which she had.

"I will help with a Z$1, to make it Z$3. Surely, that can take you to where ever you are going." The man suggested.

"This Z$2 is not mine. It has a traditional purpose to serve, *brother*," Netsai replied.

"Traditional purpose to serve?" the young man was puzzled.

"It's called *gupuro*, a divorce token. I have just been divorced by my husband, so I will need to present it to my parents otherwise they will not believe me or accept me back," Netsai said. She found herself divulging the details of her matrimonial problems. What she wanted at that moment was a listening ear and sympathy.

"Divorce token!" the young man was surprised to hear that. "Can't you just explain to your parents that you used the money for transport? Surely they must understand, rather than to put yourself in danger like this?"

Netsai laughed, another laughter mixed with sorrow. She realised that the man was too young to understand that a divorce token was to be delivered to her parents; otherwise they would not believe her.

"Let me walk, my *brother*. Thank you for the water," Netsai was a very reserved person but here she was talking about her problems to strangers, confirming the old adage: if your ancestors give you a wound, they want the flies to lick your wounds. Netsai began to walk. She was prepared to die with the Z$2 than to use it and be chased away by her parents.

When she was a few yards away, getting swallowed into the darkness of the night that seemed to be growing darker with every step she took, the young man felt a surge of pain and sympathy and decided to run after Netsai. He didn't care about the security of his own job anymore. He was concerned about this desperate woman, so he ran after her.

Netsai heard footsteps of someone running behind her. She nearly wet herself, but when she heard the voice of the young man calling her, she felt relieved because she was still debating in her mind if she was doing the right thing to walk all alone at night, and still maintain her resolve to reach home with the $2 intact.

"Why have you bothered yourself? I can walk," she said.

"Mmm, sister, I will not live with a clear conscience if I hear that you were murdered when I could have helped you. I will feel guilty for the rest of my life."

"Thank you, *brother*. What is your name?"

"Oh, sister, I am called Tendai, but people call me *Tindos*, or just *Tindo*." Netsai laughed.

"Don't you think that *Tindos* is a good name, my sister?"

"Haa it's a nice name," they laughed and walked in silence.

"But I still don't see any reason why your husband chased you away at night. Couldn't he wait and do it tomorrow during the day? Your husband is a cruel bastard!" Tendai was angry. He felt as if what Herbert had done to Netsai, had been done to his own sister.

"Ah, it's difficult to explain," Netsai shrugged her shoulders, in resignation to her fate.

"I want us to get to that bus stop where my friends drive some of those mini-buses. I will ask them to give you a free lift into town. They will also help you to get transport to Mufakose. My friends are very understanding," Tendai mixed Shona with slang, which was expected of his age. Netsai and Tendai did not see the driver who was driving slowly behind them, until he stopped the car in front of them.

Netsai was surprised; Tendai, oblivious to what was happening, stopped walking as well and watched. The driver of the car got out, and began to shout at Netsai and the young man. He did not bother to switch off the engine.

"So this is your boyfriend? You idiot of a bitch!" Herbert was walking towards Netsai angrily. Netsai did not reply.

"I have caught you red handed with a young boyfriend. Do you have anything to say? Hopeless woman. Here I am, thinking I am married to a proper woman, little do I know that you are a prostitute?"

"This young man was only walking me into safety, Herbert because these roads are dangerous; too many thieves," Netsai tried to explain to Herbert.

"You think I am a fool?" Herbert turned his attention towards Tendai. "Young man, you will die for nothing if you are not clever," he said as he grabbed Tendai by the collar. But Tendai, sensing danger, quickly broke loose from Herbert's grip and ran away back to the basket market. Herbert, who wanted to teach Tendai a lesson, ran after him. Netsai saw an opportunity present itself. Realising that the car's engine was still running with the ignition keys on, she hurriedly got into the car and drove away to Mufakose. She sped to Mufakose, fearing that Herbert might find a way to come after her.

Herbert did not realize what had just happened; he was obsessed with beating the guy he was accusing of being his wife's lover.

"Help! Help!" Tendai called out. The men who worked at the service station heard his plea and stopped what they were doing in order to find out what was happening to their friend. Herbert saw a group of men coming to him and quickly turned towards his car, but the men took up chase. There was an unwritten code of comradeship among the night watchmen, and Herbert had under-estimated that comradeship. The men stuck together in times like these.

"What are you trying to do to one of us?" one of the men asked. Herbert was now cornered by the pursing men, their fists clenched. Some had armed themselves with logs. Herbert smelt danger, but did not know what to do. He tried to find a weak spot to escape through, but there was none. He whimpered.

"You know guys; I was only trying to help that woman who came to my stall looking haggard and tired, the one I fetched water for from the garage. I was escorting her to safety to protect her from getting mugged or killed at that danger spot over there, and then what happens? I see this idiot stop a car in front of me and the woman. He then starts accusing me of having an affair with his wife," Tendai explained.

"Tindo, did I not ask you when you came to fetch water, did I not ask you where this woman was coming from at this time of the night?" the garage attendant, who was a huge man, asked Tendai.

"She is my wife. We had a small misunderstanding so I was...." Herbert did not finish his lies because Tendai interrupted.

"Misunderstanding? What kind of misunderstanding are you on about, which makes you misunderstand everyone and everything? You idiot of a man who chases away a wife in the middle of the night. I am going to beat you and teach you a lesson! Next time when you have a misunderstanding with your wife again, take her to where you want her to go, instead of endangering her life," Tendai clenched his fists and walked towards Herbert.

"It's not true, she fled from the house. I did not chase her away, that's why I was looking for her when I saw you," Herbert tried to explain, but unconvincingly. He wanted to invoke sympathy from the angry group, but he did not finish what he wanted to say because Tendai had punched him on the cheek. As he staggered to one side trying to maintain his balance, he was greeted by another fist from one of the other men. Tendai took the opportunity to flare his friends' anger by explaining how cruel Herbert was.

"This man is a liar. He gave his wife Z$2 as a divorce token. That woman showed it to me. She was even scared to use the money to pay the kombi driver because she wanted to show her parents the pathetic token."

"You stone-age man! Who told you that these days you give a wife a divorce token to break up with her? Where do you live, and which era do you belong to? Don't you know there are courts where you can seek a divorce? Did you marry her under a Muchakata tree, or inside a church or Magistrate's court? What is Z$2? It's not even enough for her bus fare. Why did you not hire a taxi for her and make sure she reaches her parent's home safely?" The muscled man hit Herbert hard on the face. He winced in pain. But that did not stop the men from hitting him again, especially after they learnt about his cruelty towards his wife. Herbert, the wife-beater, had found his own match. In his male-chauvinistic world that his mind existed, it had not occurred to him that not all men were wife-beaters.

"Where is the wife of this fool?" one older man, who did not want Herbert's beating to end up nasty, asked.

He had noticed that the woman in question was nowhere to be seen.

"Yes, she is no longer here," one man said, spitting in Herbert's face while he said, "you idiot, now look, you make us abandon our jobs because of your stupidity," he finished his sentence by kicking Herbert at the back. They looked for Netsai everywhere, but did not find her. They were now worried for Netsai's safety than they were for their wares.

"I am now worried for her. Maybe she took the risk and continued to walk to town, while we were beating this idiot," Tendai said.

Then they heard Herbert bawling like a knife had gone through his flesh. They saw him limping, searching pockets and bending over the grass. Upon realizing that the car was gone, he bawled like a crazy man.

"My car has been stolen! My car has been stolen!" Herbert was wailing. He was looking for his car keys everywhere, turning his pockets inside out, bending over the grass, looking for keys in the grass. The men went to find out what was going on.

"All you can think of is a car, and not the precious life of your wife? The car deserves to be stolen," they chorused while poking him on the forehead.

"Let us just hope the woman is safe," one guy said.

"Maybe *Amai*Farai took the car away since I left the keys in the engine," Herbert said aloud, after he realised that he had left the engine on.

"Then she is a very clever woman if she did that," one guy said, laughing at Herbert.

"If it's her, then I am going to the police to report her because she is as good as any thief," Herbert was limping, walking towards a police station. The men broke into a raucous laughter.

"You are laughing at me? I am also going to report you for assault," Herbert was shouting, his safety reassured by a group of people coming towards them.

"Go, who cares? You think the police are idiots? They can see that they are dealing with a crazy man!" Tendai said. The guys returned back to their work stations, while Herbert went to the nearest police post.

Netsai arrived at her aunt's house and parked the car at the roadside. She knocked at *Tete*Susan's door and the old woman was shocked to see her niece knocking at her door at that time of the night.

"What is it again? Is everything alright?" She asked her niece.

"*Tete*, I don't know what to do now. I really don't know!" Netsai said, trying to adjust to the light that had just been turned on.

"What happened?"

"*Tete*, this is the divorce token." Netsai showed her aunt the Z$2. *Tete*Susan shook her head in disbelief.

"You kids, why do you play with our minds like this? What is this?" she asked as she examined the money.

"I can't take this any more, *Tete*" Netsai said. "Is *Va*Simon here, I want to ask him to bring the car into the yard?" Netsai asked her aunt. "My life is now a burden to bear," she continued.

"No, your *Babamukuru* is not here," *Tete*Susan said. Netsai looked relieved, to her aunt's surprise.

"That's better, aunty. Herbert caught me red-handed with the love concoction you gave me. He went really mad. That's why he gave me *gupuro,* the divorce token." Netsai finished talking whilst fidgeting on the chair.

"So what did you tell him, I mean what explanation did you give him?" *Tete*Susan asked.

"I never got the chance to explain anything; Herbert didn't want to hear any of it."

"So where is the concoction?" *Tete*Susan inquired.

"He took it. I couldn't take it away from him because he was chasing me like a dog," Netsai explained.

"If you did not say anything to him, then that's good for us. We just tell him that it's a mixture for period pains and the other type is for cleaning the stomach. It's easy," *Tete*Susan was relieved and more confident.

"And if he asks me where I got it, what do I say?"

"I gave you. Is that a problem? Aunts always help their nieces to get the right *muti* for any ailments. There is nothing unusual about that," *Tete* said. "In fact, we can deny that the concoction he has is the one he took from you, that is, if it has to go to the village court. I think Herbert is an idiot! He doesn't want people who treat him with some respect! In me he has found a match. I will outmanoeuvre him," *Tete*Susan was angry at Herbert. If Herbert was there, she would have punched him.

"*Tete*, there's more to the story. This car that I came with, I stole it from him...."

"How?"

Netsai explained everything that had happened to her that night, up until Herbert was chasing Tendai and how she took the opportunity to get into the car and drive away safely.

"You mean you walked all that distance from your house to the craft market? How can Herbert be so mean!" *Tete*Susan was amazed by her niece's courage and repulsed by Herbert's cruelty and selfishness.

"I am going to teach that idiot husband of yours a lesson. Did you get to eat anything?" *Tete* asked.

"There was no time for all that."

*Tete*Susan made a quick meal for Netsai, who ate ravenously.

"Tonight your father must accept you because you have the divorce token that he keeps talking about," *Tete*Susan said as Netsai ate.

"Maybe he will receive me only when I am a corpse, after I am murdered by Herbert," she replied.

"At least you came with the car, otherwise how were we going to get to your parent's house?" *Tete* said.

"I am not even aware what time it is now, *Tete*. So many things have happened this evening, leaving me confused."

"It's after eleven already, we need to move."

They got into the car and left for Netsai's parents' house. *Tete*Susan explained everything that had happened. She finished by showing them the divorce token. To their surprise, Netsai's father broke into a raucous laughter.

*Tete*Susan was angered by her brother's lack of emotion.

"You are the one who said you can only take Netsai back when she is presented with a divorce token, now here she is, and she brings you the token and you sit and laugh!"

"Netsai, tell me my daughter, what are you really up to? You are so keen on getting a divorce. And you, my sister, you are a daughter of the soil who knows all our customs. What is Z$2? Anyone can just claim it's a token given to them for divorce. How do you know if this Z$2 is not some money she fished from her wallet, hmmn? We all know that *gupuro*, is only given in the presence of a witness. Where is the witness?"

"If you think she gave herself the divorce token, simply because she wants to stay unmarried, I am the aunt who can find out!" *Tete*Susan was angry.

Netsai's mother, who had been quiet all along, sizing up her husband's reaction, took the opportunity to reproach Netsai, who she thought was only up to disgrace her reputation.

"*Tete*Susan, let's not be made fools by this daughter who wants to go astray and turn into a whore. Where have you seen a man who no longer loves his wife, give her a car? Netsai has indicated before that she doesn't wish to remain married to Herbert. That's what she is up to. Don't waste our time Netsai. We are too old to go through your silly tricks," Netsai's mother was now ranting with anger. *Tete*Susan tried to explain what had really happened that evening, but her words fell on deaf ears. Netsai and her aunt left the two crazed parents, and on the way back to her aunt's house, Netsai was driving very fast because she was very angry.

CHAPTER Twelve

Herbert pressed a criminal and an assault charge at the police station. The policeman dealing with his case took Herbert in the car and they drove to *Tete*Susan's place, where Herbert knew Netsai would be.

The police officer asked Netsai to explain what had happened, and after he realised that it was a domestic issue, he decided to counsel the two.

"You were very wrong to chase your wife out of your matrimonial home without sufficient money to get home to her parents. Anything could have happened. We deal with a lot of cases of missing people, murder cases, rape cases and theft cases. If you want to divorce your wife, the same courts where you were married can grant you with a divorce, not this divorce token you are talking about. What you did was very unlawful and it amounts to domestic violence. I will let you off the hook tonight, but if you ever do such a thing again, you will be charged under the country's laws on domestic violence. And about your assault charges against the night watchmen, you can proceed with it if you want, but you must know that you provoked them, you started a fight in their territory, they did not come to your house to attack you, and so the law of self-defence will most likely apply. Think carefully before you proceed," the officer said.

Herbert realized that he would not get anywhere with the charges and dropped them. He decided to seek treatment for the injuries he had sustained from the beatings. He also realised that even if he were to press charges, he would not be able to identify any one of the men who had beaten him. They would certainly make a fool out of him and probably that would end in more retribution from the men.

"Ok, I will leave you two to sort out your problems in an amicable way," the officer said as he put the cap-of-power back on his head. All along it had been resting on his knee as he talked.

"What about the car theft charges?" Herbert asked. He had not seen the car in *Tete*Susan's yard when they arrived in the police car.

"I have the car, Herbert," Netsai said. "It's my car don't forget that. I gave it to you to use when yours broke down, so now you must go and fix your own car and I keep what belongs to me," Netsai felt empowered by the policeman's words. She now knew that there were many people who cared for vulnerable people like her, even though her old-fashioned parents were hard nuts to crack.

The officer left. He had dealt with many cases of domestic violence.

Realising that his macho-man power base was weakened, Herbert tried to beg *Tete*Susan for forgiveness but she did not give in without a fight. Eventually she spoke to Netsai and begged her to go home. However, *Tete*Susan kept the Z$2, because she was now the witness since Herbert had not denied giving Netsai the divorce token. *Tete*Susan made Herbert to sign a paper accepting that he had given Netsai *gupuro*, a divorce token. She copied the serial number of the money and attached the two dollar note to the signed document. She also wrote the date and made Herbert write in his own hand writing. She even went to the extent of asking him to put his identity card number.

Herbert spent the whole week behaving well and spending more time at his home with Netsai. He was cunning because all he wanted was to get the car back from Netsai. He appealed to Netsai to forgive his union with Aida, which he admitted was a mistake.

"When she gives birth, I will come back home and be with you all the time. At the moment, she is vulnerable because of the pregnancy, so I can not abandon her as she is carrying my blood, Farai and Tariro's blood as well," he said.

He did not want Netsai to press charges for domestic violence. Before the end of the week, Herbert had the car. Netsai had given him the car hoping that things were going to change as Herbert had promised. During the second week, Herbert came home after midnight, and after the third week, he stopped coming home altogether. It is indeed true that a leopard's spots cannot be changed. Aida had given Herbert an ultimatum, to be with her or go and live with Netsai.

Netsai was hurt. Most of her friends seemed to have abandoned her and openly talked about her predicament. She appealed to family members and church people for help, but every one of them seemed to accept that male promiscuity was a thing many married women should live with and accommodate.

"All men are like that, why do you think your case is any different from what we all go through?" they chided her.

One day Netsai decided to seek guidance from Father Ross, a white Roman Catholic Priest.

"Greetings, Mrs Kudzingwa," he said. "You have not been attending mass regularly these days as you used to do before, what is the problem? Actually, I was contemplating coming to see you at home to find out what is happening," he said.

"It's true, Father. I have been faltering," Netsai replied, before she sighed and sat down. "We just got straight into conversation, Father, before I enquired about your health. How are you, Father?"

"I am very well, Mrs Kudzingwa. How are you, the children and your husband? Especially Farai, whom I last saw during the school holidays, when he was helping with Mass. He is such a fine clever young man. Is he enjoying school?"

"He is well. He likes school and playing basketball especially," Netsai replied.

"He is a well-mannered young man, who wants to do God's work," the priest said.

"It's true, and I wish he keeps like that," Netsai said. The priest could see through Netsai's eyes that something was eating her up.

"We will bring his name before the Lord, we always pray for these young people so that God can give them guidance. It is very important for you parents to keep your faith in God very strong. You must keep coming to Church so that your children will grow up in God's love. I last saw your husband last year, is he still in this town?"

"Yes, Father...." she kept quiet for a while, took a deep breath before proceeding, "that is the reason I am here Father, to get your advice and guidance. My husband does not live with me anymore. He has moved in with another woman. That is why I have come to you Father. Each time I close my eyes to pray, I see this woman's image in front of me."

"My daughter-in-Christ, men are like children who easily get carried away by useless things. When he is finished playing his games, he will come back to you. Don't worry yourself too much, remember, you are God's child. You must keep praying and you must know that a clever woman does not destroy her house, but does everything she can to build it and keep it together. She does not compete with her husband but humbles herself before him."

"Father, what bothers me a lot is that we have a civil marriage which does not permit him to have another wife. I am thinking of going to the courts to sue him and his new wife...."

"A believer in Christ does not do that, just as a clever woman will not do that as well," the priest said. "As I said, a man is like a child, if you keep nagging him because of his wrong doings, he will move out of the house. All you need to do is to keep quiet and pray."

"What is also bothering me is that he is living with this woman in a house which I bought with my own money. If he lived with her somewhere else, I would not hurt that much. But for me to work for another woman, I find it very hard to accept."

"My child, you can still work and get more as long as you have both hands. You can still buy another house. God can make that possible, since He is the one who made it possible in the first place. As long as you are still alive, you can work and do it. Let's kneel and pray."

How can Father say that I can still work and buy another house? A body gets tired even if the mind is willing to continue working. It's time for me to rest and enjoy the fruit of my hard work, and not to start working all over again. Even God would not want me to work for others. What kind of God would want me to work for other women? It is said your ancestors don't open up opportunities twice for you. If I lose what I have now, I will never get the chance to acquire new properties.

"I will come to your house to pray there as well," the priest said as he rose from the carpet where he was kneeling. Netsai left the priest's office and walked towards her house. But her thoughts were troubling her.

She was worried.

She walked towards her house, but changed her mind and instead went to the main road and took a bus to town, then proceeded to go to Kambuzuma; to Lameck' and his wife's house.

"Welcome, my sister. You come this time of the day, when do you expect us to have more time to sit and talk?" *Amai*Rujeko asked, because it was nearly late in the afternoon, when Netsai arrived.

"I have come to spend the night here. Or are you dismissing me already?" Netsai joked. They both laughed as they got into the house.

"How are you, *Amaiguru?*" Netsai enquired, softly clapping her hands.

"I am well, if you are well, *Amainini.*"

They inquired about how the families were, before Netsai got into the purpose of her visit.

"How is *Babamudiki* Herbert? He is no longer visiting us. Did you ban him from coming here?"

"Ah, leave me alone, *Amaiguru.*" Netsai sighed, restlessly.

"Yes, we have not seen him for ages. It's not nice to lock your husband in the house," she teased Netsai.

"You are better off asking the woman he is now living with. I know nothing about his whereabouts or movements anymore," Netsai said.

"Don't tell me he is still misbehaving!"

"It's true *Amaiguru.* I am now fed up with him. Sometimes he stays at home, but spends very little time with us and children, and then he disappears for many days again."

"If he wants polygamy, then he certainly doesn't know how to handle it!" *Amai*Rujeko said. She went to sit closer to Netsai, who was repeating that she didn't know what to do anymore.

"I think his main problem is that his family is too small, so he can find time to do what he wants. Three children only! That's a very small family to tie a man to you," *Amai* Rujeko said and laughed.

Netsai did not like that kind of talk, but she suppressed her displeasure.

"How can you say that Herbert needs a more challenging family, when his son, Farai, is in school today only because he received a scholarship? What is the purpose of having many children when he can not pay fees for his son?"

"That's why, because he has only three children to support."

"What are you saying?" Netsai could not understand what her sister-in-law was implying.

131

"What I am saying is that when a family is rich, with plenty of money to spend like yours, there is need for the wife to have many children. Don't you see how my husband does not play around with money because he has a lot of mouths to feed, so he won't take any chances by having girlfriends. Where would he get the extra money to feed the girlfriends with?"

"You think so?"

"I mean it. *Babamudiki* Herbert has too much money to spend; therefore he looks for other women to sponsor. I suggest you fall pregnant quickly since he is still coming to your house. If you are still sharing the same bed, do it now"

"*Amaiguru*, I don't agree with you," Netsai did not hide her disgust.

"Don't think I am joking, my sister, because I've heard a lot about the things that were bought for this Aida woman by Herbert. It all points to one thing, that *Babamudiki* Herbert is really looking forward to a new child." *Amai*Rujeko had forgotten that she had professed ignorance about Herbert's 'small house'. Now she was talking about Herbert and Aida with an 'I know about it all' confidence.

"So, you knew all along about this small house?" Netsai felt betrayed.

"I heard about it a long time ago, but I just didn't know how to bring it up to you because I didn't want to hurt you. When I heard it, I was hurt, and I could only imagine that if it hurt me that much, what about you? That's why I was waiting for you to say it first," *Amai*Rujeko explained.

"Who told you?"

"Who else, apart from our two-faced mother-in-law? She was here last week, and.... did she not come to see you and the children? The way she praised Aida! She accused me of being on your side, and went on to say that even if I support you, Herbert is now committed to Aida and that l would have to accept that fact. She told me Aida's pregnancy scan showed that she is expecting twin boys," AmaiRujeko used gestures to emphasise her point. "So my sister, this woman, Aida, is expecting twins."

"She is already visiting Aida? You know what she said to me when I went to the village to tell her about Herbert's behaviour? She professed ignorance about Aida! You know what, people can conveniently forget about certain things. I built a house for her, the very house she lives in today, even when Herbert, her own son, did not want to have anything to do with it. And now she has forgotten all that; I am now the bad person. That's why they say if you spoil a dog by feeding it on milk everyday, that won't stop it from biting you in future."

"That's the truth, my sister. The same people you feed today, tomorrow they will laugh at you when you are in need. You cannot be a saint. Help people only a little; otherwise you just waste your resources. Now see where your sympathy has taken you! You thought we did not want to help *Amai*? We wanted to help her as well, but her character just made us apply brakes on how much we could do for her. Recently, she was saying that you are spending Herbert's money on your relatives. My husband reminded her that you were the major bread winner in your household and not Herbert."

"You know, I am at a loss for words. I don't know what to say anymore." Netsai was now feeling let down by the people she had helped before, especially her mother-in-law. The fact that Aida was expecting twins did not make it any easier for her.

"Do what I told you. Have another baby, or the other thing we can do is use a strong *muti* to tie her womb, so that she won't give birth to those babies. I can take you to a *n'anga* who leaves nearby. She has powerful *muti that* can sort that woman out!" *Amai* Rujeko said, pointing towards the direction of the traditional-healer's house with her index finger. Netsai shook her head mildly, but AmaiRujeko would not have any of it. She convinced Netsai to fight for what was rightfully hers rather than give in to her rival. They left the house to go to the famous *n'anga*'s place with *Amai*Rujeko taking the lead.

When they arrived, they removed their shoes and got inside the house. *Amai*Rujeko, who seemed to be on familiar terms with the *n'anga*, explained the reason for the visit. She referred to the *n'anga* as *Ambuya*, since the spirit medium that *possessed* her belonged to an old great-grandmother to her.

"Take this string-chord, here, take the other end," *Ambuya* said, handing Netsai a piece of string pulled from the bark of a tree.

Netsai, shaking with fear, took the string.

"Now, tie it into a knot, and at the same time say out your wish, what you want to happen to this woman," the *n'anga* explained.

Netsai did as what she was told, but her voice was barely audible.

"Speak aloud, and say what you want to happen to this woman, my roots are powerful, and your wish will be granted," the *n'anga* reiterated.

"Aida, I want you to..., I want you to...." Netsai went numb. She did not know what to say.

"What do you want to happen to her? Do you want her to die in child-birth, or do you want the babies to be still-born? Say what you want!" The *n'anga* wiped a strand of spittle that had formed on the edges of her lips with the back of her hand.

"Yes, that's what I want," Netsai said, happy that someone had said the words and not herself, thus saving her the agony of wishing evil on other people.

"Say it then, as you tie a knot with the string, say, Aida, I want you to die, or Aida, I want you to have a still-birth, do it," the woman was demonstrating.

Netsai, visibly shaking, took the string from the *n'anga*, "Aida, I want to.... I want you to....," Netsai gave up.

She put the string on the mat and shook her head.

"My sister, you take everything lightly! You think Aida is not visiting every living *n'anga* in this country, and probably wishing for worse things to happen to you? You think your situation is a joke?" *Amai*Rujeko was now losing patience with Netsai. Even the n'anga was also growing in anger.

"Don't waste my time, young woman. I am a very busy *doctor* with lots of patients. Did you come here just to check my powers?" the *n'anga* looked from Netsai to *Amai* Rujeko, seething with anger.

Netsai felt a surge of strength, took the string and sighed before she said, "Aida, I want to tie your womb, so that both you and your unborn babies die," she took a deep breath again.

"Take the string and place it at Aida's door step, or anywhere in her yard. Then take the other one to your house, tie it somewhere and wet it with water everyday, and use the water in the bottle that I will give you. Each time you sprinkle the water, say your wishes aloud, what you want to happen to this Aida as you have just done now," the *n'anga* handed Netsai a small brown bottle with a clear liquid inside it.

"*Ambuya*, I am afraid of going to this woman's house. What will happen if she finds me walking around the yard?" Netsai was really worried.

"You can ask your sister here to take it there for you. I am sure she will want to help you just as she has demonstrated by bringing you to me," the *n'anga* said.

*Amai*Rujeko agreed to go to Milton Park. They paid for their services and quickly left the *n'anga's* house. They did not say goodbye because saying so was believed to render the *muti* less effective.

While Netsai and her sister-in-law were consulting the services of a *n'anga*, Herbert was sitting in a hospital room at Avenues Clinic, admiring his bundles of life in a cot-bed by Aida's bedside. A midwife walked in.

"Is it normal for babies born nearly six hours ago, not to be able to open their eyes?" Herbert asked the midwife.

"It's very normal. They are just tired," the midwife responded as she prepared to wheel the cots into the nursery.

"You know what darling? You have really made me a proud father, a man among men to have twin boys. I don't know how else I am going to thank you," Herbert said. "Tell me your wish, and I will grant it straight away."

"You know what you can do for me and the boys, is to register the Milton Park house in our names. You never know what may happen tomorrow. I don't want to end up homeless with these two boys I brought to life for you. They need assurance that they will be well looked after, that Farai, your eldest son and heir, won't take away everything from them."

Aida, who had been raised up by a grandmother in a polygamous setting, knew how harshly property rights affected the woman out of wedlock, or the younger wife in polygamy. Her grandmother, who was the second wife in the marriage, inherited nothing from her husband after Aida's grandfather died. All the property was inherited by the eldest son, who was tasked with looking after all the siblings. Polygamy was not new to her and she did not have a whim about being someone's second wife. She believed that she had taken after her grandmother. As long as she played her cards right, she had no fear of suffering the same plight as her grandmother.

"Farai? Why do you talk about Farai? I don't want him to inherit anything. He is an idiot of a son. A son who always takes his mother's side each time an argument ensues? Idiot of a boy!" Herbert was getting angry.

"He is your son, please don't say that," Aida said. Herbert screwed his face in disgust.

"So what do you say about my wish?" Aida asked Herbert, looking him straight in the eyes so as to be able to gauge his response.

"That's a small request. Consider your wish granted. I want my boys to inherit my wealth, and when you get discharged, we will go to the Deeds Office and add your name on the title deeds."

"Thank you very much, darling. Now I don't have to worry about the future of my children. That's a lifetime present. I will thank you well when I leave the hospital." Aida drew Herbert closer to her and planted a kiss on his lips. Herbert was thrilled.

"It's nothing, darling. It's something, which every father should do for his children. I love my children and want them to have what they should. Even if you had not asked me to do it, I was going to do it out of a fatherly duty." He kissed Aida on the lips and caressed her cheeks. After a while, he bade her farewell because he wanted to go to the village to collect his mother. He was in a celebratory mood.

Aida was pleased with Herbert's response. She was already looking forward to being a homeowner. Overcome with happiness, she pinched herself a few times to make sure she was not daydreaming. She wanted to jump out of the bed and break into a dance, but realized she was still tired after pushing out two big babies into the world. She began to talk, but to no one in particular.

"It's true; Herbert is going to register the Milton Park house in my name. All along I didn't know how to bring up this issue, thinking that he might just see me as a gold-digger, but it seems I was wrong. *Vakuru vakati mwana asingacheme anofira mumbereko.* A child who does not cry can die quietly on his mother's back, without the mother realising that the child is dead. I am a very lucky woman. If he does that, I am the winner. Nothing to fear anymore! I can sit and relax, do whatever I want, because I have won the jackpot."

CHAPTER Thirteen

When Netsai left her sister-in-law, she did not go home straight away, but decided to go and see her friend Rhoda, whom she had not seen for a long time.

"Umm, Netsai, why are you so scarce these days?" Rhoda asked.

"Too many things to do my friend. I wasn't even sure that I would find you at home. I just decided to take a chance," Netsai replied, sitting on the chair offered by her friend.

"These days I have decided to work from home, so I converted one of my rooms into a sewing room. My customers know where to find me. I don't really need to work from a central place in the city anymore. I take my orders on the phone, make the things and deliver them to the people. Are you still operating your business from the city? I think it's a waste of money to pay rent when you can work from home," Rhoda said.

"Yes, I am still renting a shop in town, but the business is not doing very well. I am going through a very difficult patch in life," Netsai said. Her voice sounded weak and tired.

"What do you mean your business is not doing well? If a veteran like you cries foul, what about small fish like us, juniors in the industry?"

"That is over, my friend. Things change. My life is not in a good shape at the moment. I am only left with one assistant, the others left since I could no longer afford to pay them."

"It must be pretty hard for you then, if it has got to the point that you are failing to pay your workers. What is happening Netsai?"

"My husband caused all this mess I am in. He used to go to the shop and take all the money from my business until we got destitute."

"Don't tell me!" Rhoda was shocked to hear that.

"Yes, my friend, Herbert was doing that. He is living a double life, that's why."

"What do you mean he is living two lives?"

"Herbert has another wife. If you come to my house you will be surprised to find that our living standard has deteriorated. It's very difficult to comprehend. I sold the two mini-buses because Herbert was taking money from the drivers. He did not care that the drivers needed to be paid from the daily takings, and that the buses needed regular servicing. I had no choice but to sell them." Tears welled in her eyes when she said those words.

"What you are telling me is news, Netsai. I am at a loss as to what to say. You were one of the couples that everyone admired, and now to turn to this!"

"What eats me most is that Herbert is living with his 'small house' in our Milton Park house, can you believe it?" Rhoda just shook her head." You know how hard this sewing business is. I have permanent scars from needle pricks, and the sleepless nights that we endure for us to finish orders on time. All of that effort, to pay for another woman's comfort and luxuries!.,"

Netsai was very emotional.

"How could he put his new wife in your house? Did you not jointly buy the properties?" Rhoda wanted to get to the bottom of the matter.

"You know, I was a fool blinded by love. I did not bother to have my name on either of the houses, and now that you have asked me that question, I remember when we bought the houses, the secretary at the estate agent's office sincerely advised me to have my name on the title deeds. At the time I thought she was one of those single women who wanted to spoil it for others. I saw it as jealous talk."

"Netsai, are you serious? Do you know Herbert can sell those houses without you knowing if you are not careful? How could you do such a thing, letting him have sole-ownership of three houses?"

"I was blinded by love...."

"Women must wake up, love is not blind. Why is it that love is blind to women only? Men fall in love with their eyes wide open. You should know that by now! Everything you do, you must do it with your eyes open, except for sleeping of course, but even then, people dream in sleep as well," she sighed. "You can't just give the fruits of your hard work to Herbert on a silver platter. All those days of going to South Africa to buy things to re-sell, and you let him take everything?"

Netsai nodded her head in agreement, as she too, remembered the difficult years of hard work.

"Listen, Netsai, let me give you a business card of a lawyer called Nancy Rusero. My young sister had a similar problem like yours, and this lawyer sorted out everything for her. Her husband was in the process of selling their house without her knowledge, and the lawyer applied for an injunction order through the High Court. Now both their names appear on the title deeds. Her husband is behaving well now, you can't even tell that he was the same person who wanted to sell the house," Rhoda said as he fished out the lawyer's business card from her purse.

"I will go and see this lawyer tomorrow before things turn nasty for me." Netsai took the card and put it in her bag.

"You need to act fast. You know with our parents' houses it was better, those City Council houses we grew up in, in Mbare Township were registered in the husband and wife's name. Those houses were only allocated to them on the basis of marriage. Don't you remember that famous story about a prostitute who was chased out of the house during one of the Council's inspection rounds because they discovered she was not the woman whose name was on their register? That was really good."

Netsai and Rhoda laughed. Netsai had grown up in Mbare were her parents had a house and Rhoda was her friend from childhood. In the late 1970's the parents moved to Marimba Park.

"Even though residents in council-owned houses did not like those inspections; I really didn't like them myself, but they saved a lot of marriages since a lot of wives spent long periods of time farming in the rural areas," Rhoda continued. "Because of title deeds, a lot of women lose their houses when the husband sells the house or simply add some other woman's name on the deeds."

"You are right, my friend. What you said has really opened my eyes and ears. I shall not stay here any longer. I want to go home and make an appointment with this lawyer," Netsai was already getting up from the chair. She felt a lot better after talking to Rhoda.

"Let me give you something to eat before you go." Rhoda went into the kitchen straight away, and not taking no for an answer, brought two glasses, a bottle of cold drink and two pieces of roasted chicken. Netsai ate very little. Even though she was hungry; her mind was somewhere else.

"You need to eat because this battle you are fighting needs a lot of energy. You look very thin. It's not good for you," Rhoda advised her friend.

"I have done much better today. Where can one get the appetite when you have heavy problems on your shoulders?" Netsai finished her drink and stood up. Since it was getting dark Rhoda gave Netsia a lift to go home.

Netsai arrived home and tied the string that she had been given by the *n'anga* on one of the trees in her yard. She sprinkled it with the prescribed water. She performed the ritual as she had been instructed. The tree was very close to her laundry lines, where the family hanged the clothes to dry. She decided to collect the clothes that were hanging on the laundry lines to relieve Tsitsi, and for a while forgot about the string. Her leg was trapped by the string and she fell forwards, hitting her face on a tree stump. She began to bleed. She was in pain and so angry that she took a knife, cut the string off the tree and threw it away.

"I have not always believed in these things, now it's as if I brought a curse on my life." She went to the bathroom and cleaned her injury.

"What were you doing outside, mama that made you bleed?" Tsitsi asked.

"Collecting the laundry. I fell, but don't worry, let me rest, my dear," Netsai said, fetching some bandages from the medicine cupboard.

"I think you are worrying yourself too much, that's why you fell like that." Tsitsi was worried.

"You are right, Tsitsi, I am thinking too much. It's not good for me."

*Amai*Rujeko went to Milton Park straight away, after she left the *n'anga's* house with Netsai. But when she got to the house, she nearly bumped into Herbert who was returning back from the village where he had gone to fetch his mother. As Herbert's car approached the gate, *Amai*Rujeko took cover behind the hedge. She decided to throw the string into the yard from the position she was hiding. She did, and got into the taxi she had hired and sped from the scene. She was worried about whether she had done the right thing or not. She did not know yet that Aida had already given birth to twin boys that morning.

She did not know that inside the house that she had just left, Herbert's mother, *Va*Soda, was dancing with happiness, singing Aida's praise totem for giving them two boys at once. It was as if Aida's twin boys were the only grandchildren she had ever had!

Aida's mother was also in the house. It was a celebration for the two grandmothers who had other grandchildren they seemed not to care much about.

"Aida has given me the best present on this earth, two healthy *husbands*!" *Va*Soda danced and ululated. It was custom for grandmothers to refer to their grandsons as husbands, because grandsons carry the family name to posterity.

"Hukamai hunenge husahwira?
Hukamai hunenge husahwira?"

The two in-laws sang as they danced round the living room. It was difficult to believe that they were the same ladies who groaned and whimpered in pain when arthritis bit through their old bones as it so often did. When they became tired they sat down and exchanged greetings.

"I thought you would not arrive today, that's why I had gone to bed early," Aida's mother said.

"I was delayed by a funeral in our village. That's were the twins' father found me," *Va*Soda said.

"I am sorry to hear about the death in your village, *vamukurungayi*, my in-law," Aida's mother said.

"Death is our daily business these days. It's one funeral after another, maybe it is this disease that everyone is talking about. How are the boys, tell me, *vamukurungayi*, in-law, you are the one who saw them," *Va*Soda asked.

"They are very big, very big *men*, you wouldn't believe they are twins. "

The following morning Herbert, *Va*Soda and Aida's mother went to the hospital to see Aida and the twins. The old grandmothers danced in the ward and were singing as they had done the previous night, until the nurse on duty told them not to make too much noise for the other babies in the nursery. Herbert took them to Milton Park, before he drove to Estlea, to see Netsai. When he arrived at the gate, he saw the priest's car also turning into the yard. He had come to pray for the family as he had promised the day before.

"I am happy I found you both at home," the priest said, greeting Herbert.

"You are in luck today, because I don't usually come home straight after work. I usually go and meet my friends first."

"It's always good for a man to go home and see his family first, before going out," the priest said.

"You are right, Father," Herbert said, and led the Priest into the house, where the priest greeted Netsai and the children.

"What happened to your head, Mrs Kudzingwa?" the priest asked.

"I tripped on a loose wire when I went to collect the laundry outside," she replied, feeling ashamed about the real reason that had led her to trip and fall.

Herbert did not know what to say, because he did not want to show the priest that he was an absentee husband most of the time."

"You should not go outside at night," Herbert, said, feigning sympathy and concern.

"Mr Kudzingwa, I have not seen you in church for months, have you switched to another church?" the priest asked.

"I haven't changed from my church, Father."

"I asked because these days I only see your wife and children, so I thought maybe you joined another congregation," the priest said. He did not want to confront Herbert about his second wife, but wanted to bring the subject up in a clever way.

"I work out of town most of the time, and when I am in Harare I finish work very late. I wish there was a night congregation to accommodate people like me. I can not attend the evening service because I usually finish work late at night and get home around twelve midnight on many occasions," Herbert had become a habitual liar. His wife did not say anything.

"Well, I came to pray for you and your family, because I was worried about your continuous absence from the church. So let us kneel down and pray," the priest said.

They all knelt down and prayed. The priest sprinkled some holy water in the house. He bade farewell to them and left. Netsai went into the kitchen and prepared some food for Herbert. She set it on the table for him and went to the bedroom to do other things.

"Netsai, why do you give me food and then go away? When I don't stay here you complain, and when I come you ignore me, what kind of attitude is that?"

"I am sewing a dress for one of my customers," Netsai replied.

"Can you come here for a little while?" Herbert said. Netsai came into the lounge and sat down, and waited to hear what Herbert had to say. She was behaving like a schoolgirl waiting for instructions from her teacher.

"Have you eaten your supper?" Hebert asked Netsai, while drying his wet hands with a cloth before dipping them into a bowl of *sadza.*

"I have eaten already, but I can do with a small piece of meat," Netsai replied and fished out a small piece of meat from his plate.

Netsai did not want Herbert to think that she might had sprinkled the food with a love potion, or worse still, some bad concoction to make him ill. Since the incident with the *muti,* she did her best to put Herbert's mind at ease.

"*Amai*Farai, I did not want you to hear this from people because you would end up accusing me of hiding things from you," Herbert said, as he rolled a morsel of *sadza* in his hand. Netsai went pale, not knowing what bombshell Herbert was about to drop on her.

"Aida has given birth to twin boys," he rolled the morsel in beef stew and carefully put it in his mouth. He chewed it as if eating *sadza* was the most important thing to him in the world. Netsai looked at him in awe, mouth wide open and eyes unblinking. It was as if she had just been told about the death of someone she so loved.

"You heard me, didn't you? Aida has twin boys, so as the father I think this is the time both you and her made up and get to meet each other formally," Herbert said, displaying an 'I don't-care what you are thinking' attitude.

Netsai did not respond.

"What does your silence mean? Aida is ready to meet you and get to know you. Now that there are children involved it is all up to you to play the motherly role and embrace her. I want my children to grow up in harmony, knowing one another, and not for them to be divided by jealousy."

"You can bring them together, but leave me out of it. Right now I am struggling to feed my own children while you keep another woman in a house, which is supposed to give us money. Now my children's standard of living has drastically dropped because of the same woman, and you want me to embrace her? Don't you think that you have caused me enough torment, Herbert? " Netsai was shaking with anger. She didn't care anymore about Herbert's reaction.

"You are a hypocrite. You pretend to go to church and call yourself a Christian? What kind of a Christian is as ruthless as you are? You sleep at the church, praying for peace and forgiveness. What kind of peace do you bring? You are the devil Lucifer walking on this earth!" Herbert was now fuming.

"Herbert, don't you ever forget that you are using my car everyday, driving another woman in my car. You ruined your car, and you don't want to have it repaired, and now I have to beg neighbours to carry my children to school in their cars. What kind of a Christian do you need? You can do whatever you want, to please yourself and satisfy your new love, but one day the tide will turn against you."

"What will turn against me? Am I the first one to practice polygamy? You are never going to get that car back, not ever again! When I married you, did you have a car?"

Netsai did not say much more, she just left the lounge and went to bed. Herbert followed her in the bedroom, and got into bed as well. He began to caress

Netsai. She tried to push him away, but he would have none of that. He felt encouraged by her attitude; he wanted to prove to her that he was the man of the house.

"Don't you dare touch me, Herbert! You only want to satisfy your desire because your woman has just given birth. Leave me alone, please!" she begged.

"Are you not my wife as well? Do you have boyfriends to satisfy your desires? I am not going to let you off this time, you are my wife," he boasted, resting his thick hand on Netsai's bosom. They fought, until she was overpowered. Herbert forced himself on her. It was short and mechanical. When he was satisfied, much to Netsai's disgust, he rolled onto his back and began to snore. She felt violated. She woke up and washed herself before going to sit in the lounge. She was feeling dirty, and her mind was preoccupied by the fact that Aida had given birth to the twins regardless of the *n'anga's muti*. She regretted about how she had hurt herself outside when she went to collect the laundry because of the useless, stupid rope administered by the woman.

She cried. What Netsai did not know was that by the time she went to see the *n'anga*, Aida had already given birth.

Herbert followed her into the lounge.

"So why are you crying? " He asked, poking Netsai on the cheek.

"Do you know that you have just raped me, Herbert?" It was a statement rather than a question.

"You are now mad. Go and report me to the police, and we will see if they will come and arrest me for sleeping with my wife. I want to take you to the bedroom and *rape* you again as you call it. I want to teach you a lesson!" Herbert dragged Netsai to the bedroom, where he repeatedly forced himself on her.

Netsai hardly slept that night, while Herbert enjoyed tormenting her. She went to the bathroom and filled the bathtub with water and soaked her body in it.

She wanted to get rid of Herbert's smell from her body, but she found that no amount of soap and water could erase what had just happened to her. Since Herbert had began living his double life, he had hardly touched or kissed her, except during the time he had wanted to get the car back from her. But even then, the touching and kissing was mechanical and lacked emotional commitment. Netsai had reluctantly accepted her state of celibacy, until she was forced to fully accept it. Now Herbert was imposing himself on her simply to satisfy his pleasure, not bothering whether she wanted it or not, or if she was ready or not. She also knew that the rape was not the end, but would almost certainly to become routine as long as Aida was still fragile after having given birth.

Herbert was woken up by the sound of running water. He went to the bathroom.

"What does all this washing and bathing mean? Am I now something that you don't want to get close to? Do I smell? This is not the first time you have had this endless bathing." Herbert reached the plug in the bathtub and yanked it off. He was grinning all the while, just to torment Netsai and to show her that he was in charge, not her. He banged the door and walked out of the bathroom. She filled the bath up again and stayed in the water until the water became cold on her body. In the morning, she left early for her aunt's house, where, she broke into uncontrollable sobbing.

"What is it again?" her aunt asked her. "What brings you so early to my doorstep and in tears as well?"

"How can things be alright, *Tete*....?" Netsai broke down. Her aunt, who was now used to seeing her niece cry more than she laughed, patted her on her back, giving her time to regain her composure and narrate her ordeal.

"*Tete*, since Herbert began his 'small-house', he has not hurt me more than he did last night," *Tete*Susan kept quiet, waiting for her to finish. "He came home boasting about how Aida has given birth to twin boys and how I should reach out to Aida to formalise relations for the sake of our children...."

"I can't believe this!" *Tete*Susan said in disbelief.

"*Tete*, Herbert raped me, not once, but many times last night," she continued. Her aunt's mouth was agape, stunned. If she thought her aunt was surprised because Herbert had raped her, she misread her thoughts. *Tete*Susan was shocked because she had never heard a wife accuse her husband of rape. For a moment she thought Netsai had gone insane. That was why she was looking at Netsai with registered shock on her face; and not because she was shocked by Herbert's actions. Netsai felt encouraged to continue outlining her ordeal, convinced that her aunt was both supporting her and feeling sorry for her. She locked her hands on the back of her head and began to cry like a child.

"*Muzukuru*, my niece, are you still alright upstairs? Where on earth have you heard of a husband raping his own wife? All along you were complaining that he is ignoring you, and now he reaches out to you, and you accuse him of rape? How do you want him to make up with you, if not in the bedroom? Herbert paid *lobola* for you, and has every right to sleep with you whenever he feels like it. All you need to do is open your legs, and wider if it means you may have to do so," she chided her niece, whom she was almost convinced was responsible for the breakdown of the marriage.

As she was reproaching Netsai, *Tete*Susan's young sister, Bessie, arrived at the house. She was surprised to find her niece in tears, and quickly joined in the conversation.

"What is it, Netsai, my niece, that makes you cry like this?" she inquired, hugging her.

"Our niece is going mad, my young sister," *Tete* Susan replied, clapping her hands together in resignation.

"You look like you are amused by the whole thing, what is it that makes you cry and your aunt look astounded?" Bessie asked again.

"Your niece has developed these weird ideas. How can she accuse her own husband of raping her, hmmn? Have you ever heard anything like that, Bessie?"

Bessie looked at her elder sister with a reproachful eye, but did not say anything. She turned to Netsai and pulled her closer to her asking her more questions.

"Netsai, did you feel that Herbert forced you to sleep with him? Did he force himself on you?" Bessie asked.

"Aunty, Herbert forced himself on me. We fought and he overpowered me, not only once, but several times," Netsai felt that *Tete*Bessie was more understanding. She began to wail even more. Anyone would have thought that there was a funeral at the house, but the person would then wonder why it was only one person crying, while the oldest of them stood smiling with hands held akimbo, and the younger woman hugging and patting the one crying, as if rocking a baby to sleep.

"Can't you see that Netsai is traumatised? Rape is not a good thing to happen to any woman," Bessie said, looking at her sister with an eye that spoke volumes, but *Tete*Susan was still not convinced that a husband can be accused of raping his wife.

"Maybe she is possessed by one of our male ancestral spirits, which does not want other men, that is why she is behaving like this." *Tete*Susan was trying to justify her thinking. Bessie did not answer her, she took a tissue from her wallet and wiped Netsai's tears, but that did not make her stop, in fact, it fuelled the tears.

*Tete*Susan had a very low opinion of her young sister, Bessie, because she was not married. She had divorced her husband and was bringing up her children on her own. Bessie continued to rock Netsai, until she fell asleep on her lap. She then pulled a cushion from the chair and placed it under Netsai's head for comfort. She followed her sister into the kitchen where she had gone to prepare some food.

"*Amai*Francisca, my sister, if you hear a *child* like Netsai talking about these things, don't just rebuke her, you must give her a listening ear and offer words of comfort and not dismiss her as an attention seeker. Rape is not something to joke about. Some people lose their sanity after they have been raped. We all know that Herbert has been ill-treating her, both physically and emotionally, and for him to just conveniently force himself on Netsai is rape. All he could have done was to ask for forgiveness and not rape her," Bessie said.

"I am not surprised that she is learning all these strange ideas from you. What else can she learn from you other than that? You think living on your own is civilization? That is not civilization. Where have you heard of a man raping his own wife?" *Tete*Susan defended Herbert's actions.

"It's not about civilization or lost civilization. It is about doing the right thing. In our culture, a man who abandons his wife and goes astray asks for forgiveness from his estranged wife before he can join her in bed. Herbert was supposed to pay Netsai some kind of appeasement, a token, before sleeping with her. He has been violent to her, but he never paid anything to her to get her forgiveness. In some families he would not get away with it so easily, without paying a cow to ask for forgiveness from Netsai and from us," Bessie continued.

"Bessie, what kind of advice can you give me, or teach Netsai since you divorced your own husband for no reason at all? I see Netsai following your footsteps. I am only trying to help her keep her husband and dignity. We don't want her to divorce. *Tete*Susan said.

"You think there is still a relationship between them? They are no longer husband and wife, serve for that piece of paper they call a marriage certificate.

That's why I am very happy to be a single-mother. I don't have to pretend that everything is alright, that I am happy when I am not, just to please other people. If Herbert continues to behave like an animal, he will soon taste my wrath. How can he marry another wife, put her in Netsai's house without proper protocol? It's not polygamy, but prostitution, because in polygamy, the first wife plays a role in the choice and induction of the second wife into the family. Nothing is secretive," Bessie was angry.

*Tete*Susan just sighed, because she too, knew that there was truth in what Bessie was saying. However, she did not agree with her sister on the idea of a husband raping his own wife. She could not imagine her husband, coming home wanting sex and she denying him, even if she was very tired or did not feel like doing so. The world was coming to an end if a husband was to be accused of rape simply for demanding his dues from his wife, something, which is rightly his, and sanctioned through the payment of *lobola.*

"Why did he marry this second wife? Prior to his marrying a second wife, he never came to us to tell us that they were not agreeing on many things with Netsai, and that Netsai was refusing to sleep with him; he just went on to marry another woman because he can not keep his rope in his pants," Bessie fumed.

"Bessie, stop talking to me as if I am Herbert," *Tete*Susan knew that her younger sister was angry, but she did not want her to vent her anger towards herself and not Herbert.

"You accused me of abandoning my culture because I think civilisation is abandoning one's culture. I am only trying to put sense into your head, that people hide and blame foreign cultures as corrupting our minds, when we are the ones who do not even know how our own traditions work. We don't understand them, and yet we are quick to blame someone when things go wrong," Bessie liked to call a spade a spade.

"I am tired of this talk," TeteSusan retorted.

"Herbert invaded Netsai's granary without asking for her permission...."

"Which granary are you talking about now? Do you know something that I am not aware of?" TeteSusan was now puzzled.

"So what do you call Netsai's savings' account? Isn't it as good as a granary? When our ancestors harvested their crops, they kept reserves for future use in granaries. When Netsai earned her money through sewing and cross-border trading, she banked the money for future use, and isn't that just as good as a granary filled with corn for future consumption? What Herbert did is enough to warrant an avenging spirit from Netsai should she die before he settles the score," Bessie talked like a preacher. "He raided Netsai's bank account, withdrew all the money to go and pay lobola for another woman, was that right? "

"Umm, I did not realise...."

"Sister, what is the difference between what Herbert did with what our grandfather did, when he took food from grandmother Shorai to give his second wife to eat? Remember we are going to the village next week to pay a bull to appease grandmother Shorai's spirit, which has been haunting the whole family. Herbert has just done the same thing right in front of us."

TeteSusan opened her mouth. She now saw sense in what Bessie was saying. Yes, there was a similarity between what their grandfather had done, and what Herbert was doing. You don't marry another woman using resources from your first wife to feed your new wife. It was wrong for Herbert to take Netsai's money from her savings account and use it to marry another woman, without Netsai's consent.

"You know, Bessie, today you have really taught me something. I had not realised the similarity of these two scenarios," she said, shaking her head.

"I am working in this vicinity today, which is why I dropped by to see you; otherwise I need to return to work. Please, when Netsai wakes up, try to understand where she is coming from, be as supportive as you can and not chide her like she is an unruly child," Bessie said as she left the kitchen and walked towards her car. "Remember, my sister, there is *shuramatongo*, AIDS, these days. Netsai has every right to refuse to sleep with Herbert if she doesn't want to, and especially without protection. I am going."

"Ah, Bessie, you are mean. Can't you just leave me a few pennies to buy a drink?" *Tete*Susan begged, as she escorted her younger sister to the door.

"I should be asking you for money for a drink, because I am the one raising a family single-handedly as a divorcee, *mazakela*," Bessie said as she fished Z\$50 from her purse. "I am only giving you this so that you can buy my niece a drink, I don't give money to married women," Bessie joked as she handed her sister the money.

*Tete*Susan locked the door and went to buy some drinks from a tuck-shop nearby. Netsai heard her aunt lock the door. She sat up and began to talk to herself again.

"I think it's about time for me to seek legal advice. It's better for me to get my houses back, and lose Herbert, than to lose both. I can't stop Herbert from having a relationship with Aida, but it is wrong for them to live off my sweat. They can always start their own things; buy their own house with their own money. I am not as foolish as they seem to believe, and I will fight for what belongs to me," Netsai was shaking her head.

*Tete*Susan brought the cool drinks, which they drank quietly. Netsai was feeling refreshed and energized. The thought of fighting for what belonged to her re-energized her. *Tete*Susan still tried to persuade her to go back home and relax, because what Herbert had done is what most men did to their wives. But

Netsai was sick and tired of hearing this kind of passive talk. She was planning to contact the lawyer, Ms Nancy Rusero, as soon as possible.

CHAPTER Fourteen

Netsai left her home very early to go and see the lawyer, Ms Nancy Rusero. She arrived at Karigamombe Building and took a lift to the seventh floor, where she had been told the office was. She alighted from the lift amidst a stream of people who were coming into work to start their early morning duties. She saw a signpost indicating the direction to Nancy Rusero's offices. She walked to the offices and was immediately elated when she saw the words **Nancy Rusero Legal Practitioners** written on the door. She knocked and went inside. She stood facing an elegant receptionist, who smiled at her.

"Can I help you, madam?" the receptionist asked.

"Can I see the lawyer, Ms Rusero?"

"What's your name?" the receptionist asked as she checked her appointments book.

"My name is Netsai Kudzingwa."

"What time is your appointment, because your name is not written anywhere in the book?" the receptionist asked, looking at Netsai.

"I don't have an appointment. I did not make one because I had not realised that I needed to make one, please can you allow me to see her?"

Netsai was timid and looked desperate.

"You will have to wait a little longer because there are many people who have appointments with her this morning; or you can come back tomorrow, if you want. I can book you in for tomorrow."

"I think I will wait. I really need to see her. I can wait, but if I can't get to see her today, I can make an appointment for tomorrow, but for now I am happy to wait," Netsai said. Fortunately, she was lucky because someone phoned to cancel an appointment. She was the third person to see the lawyer that morning.

Netsai was ushered into the lawyer's office, where she began narrating her story. While Netsai was talking to the lawyer, Herbert was in the hospital playing with his two newly born sons.

He was all smiles.

"I inquired from the estate agent about including your name on one of the houses. He told me that we can have joint ownership. You need to come with me and sign the documents. As soon as you leave the hospital, when you are feeling strong and fit, we will go to the agent and sort out the signing of documents," Herbert said. Aida was thrilled; she could not believe her luck.   Manna from heaven was what this was to her.

"You think I can wait until I become stronger and fit? No, I can go with you any time. You can just take me in the car," Aida said.

She wanted it done before Herbert could change his mind. She was a very cunning woman, a gold digger who meant business.

"We can go as soon as you are discharged from hospital. I am planning to sell my house in Glen View so that I can use the money to top up the lawyer's fees needed to add your name to the house," Herbert said.

He was playing with one of his sons who was on his lap.

"Is it necessary to sell the house, Herbert? Don't you think we already have enough money for that?" Aida asked. She was pretending to sound reasonable, but in her heart she was happy that Netsai and her children would be stripped of any valuable properties. She meant war with Netsai, but she did not want to expose her true feelings to Herbert. Not just yet, maybe later, when she had established herself. Joint-ownership of one of the houses was the first step.

"I also want you to have your own car, as I promised. It will be good for you to drive yourself around in case something goes wrong with the boys when I am not around. I don't want you to use public transport with my sons." Herbert was sounding posh and pompous, so as to maintain the image of the businessman he had portrayed to Aida and her family. He was just an ordinary driver at work. He was willing to sell all that he had acquired with Netsai to satisfy his young wife. Aida just grinned, not believing her luck in picking a caring man like Herbert for a husband.

Herbert had been contemplating selling the house in Glen View for a long time now. He wanted to sell it for a high price since they had finished constructing it and done all the necessary renovations, when Netsai's business was at its peak. Now that he had squandered almost every penny in their savings, and had resorted to taking money from Netsai's shop, he had to sell the house as a means of getting money to support his new family.

* * *

Netsai finished narrating her case to the lawyer, Ms Nancy Rusero, who told her how she was going to deal with the case. She had studied law at the University of Zimbabwe and had specialised in family law.

"Your case is a bit complicated, but I am going to do my best to make sure that you are protected by the law and both your names are registered on all the three houses. It is a good thing that you sought advice in time, because believe it or not, there are many women facing the same dilemma as you are now. I have dealt with cases that are even more complicated than yours. In some cases I have stopped husbands from selling the houses just in time, when the house was already on the market." Nancy pressed a button, which linked her with the receptionist.

"Julia, can you phone the deeds office and connect me to Mr Chinotimba, please?" Nancy instructed her receptionist.

She turned to Netsai and continued with her conversation. "It is hard to believe that with all your hard work, you were naive enough to buy three houses in your husband's name?"

"When you are madly in love, you think everything belongs to your husband since he has the moral responsibility to provide for the family. Little did I know that things would change any time," Netsai was feeling much better after talking to Nancy. She felt reassured; whatever might happen now, the law and her lawyer would do their best to protect her.

"You worked too hard for someone to just come and enjoy the fruit of your labour without contributing anything. I always advise women that even when they are full-time housewives, when they buy houses they should make sure their names appear on the title deeds as well. Raising children and cooking for a husband is also a job." Nancy told Netsai.

She was waiting to be connected to Mr Chinotimba.

"You are right. It's ignorance that consumes us," Netsai said.

"Women's proprietary rights did not come with the new laws. If you go back to the old days, you will find out that our ancestors also respected women's rights regarding properties. When a man married a second or third wife, he had to build a new house for the new woman before bringing her into the family. It was unwritten law, unlike now where we have statutes to refer to. Love is something that can come to an end at any time, so women should always be vigilant about their rights and entitlements."

Netsai nodded her head in agreement before saying, "You are right, every woman must work for her own things and not enjoy someone's cake."

"You can not work for the rest of your life. I am not going to work as a lawyer until I die. I need to retire at some point. Everyone needs rest, that is why there is a retirement age and pensions," Nancy said.

Her phone rang and Mr Chinotimba was on the line.

"Hello Mr Chinotimba. It's Nancy Rusero again, sorry to be a bother. Can you get the records for three houses registered in Herbert Kudzingwa's name please?" Nancy gave Mr Chinotimba the addresses for the three houses.

"No, you are not bothering me. This is part of my job. I will give you a call as soon as I get hold of the records," Mr Chinotimba said.

"You can come tomorrow anytime. I think by then I would be having all the information we require at hand," Nancy told Netsai. Netsai thanked the lawyer and left, feeling much better and relieved.

She did not go home straight, but decided to go through VaGwaku's office. The offices were a stone's throw away from where she was coming from. When she got to the offices, she did not know what to say to the agent. She felt embarrassed, but finally summoned enough courage to knock on the door. Before long she was standing face to face with the same secretary she had despised when they bought the houses. The secretary recognized her, but thought better not to bother greeting her because she still remembered clearly how she had been told off by Netsai years back. Netsai understood the tension. The secretary phoned VaGwaku to notify him of the visitor, and she pointed Netsai to VaGwaku's door without saying anything.

"I haven't seen you in a long time," VaGwaku said, shaking Netsai's hand and offering her a seat. "You only come to our offices when you want to buy houses, after that, no more contact, not even to check on our health," he joked with Netsai.

"It's not like that, VaGwaku. It's just that I was very busy," Netsai replied.

"It will certainly rain today, to receive a visit from you."

"You can say that again VaGwaku, but I am really sorry to bother you," she fell silent as if to measure the gravity of what she wanted to say. "I have got a problem. You remember when we bought those two houses and you advised me to have my name registered on both houses and I didn't take your advice? Now I want to have my name registered for both houses. My life is no longer the same, *Va*Gwaku. My husband has married another wife and put her in our house in Milton Park. I am afraid that he might sell it without my consent and knowledge, so I want my name on both houses, please, if that is possible." Netsai was a very private person, but that day she found herself pouring her family problems to *Va*Gwaku.

"I won't want to lie to you; your case is very complicated. What is Herbert up to? What has gotten into Herbert's head?" He shook his head. "Anyway, let's hope he doesn't think of selling the houses. Can I phone you later today?" *Va*Gwaku asked Netsai. He was feeling sorry for Netsai, and from his behaviour it was obvious that there was something else he knew that he wanted to share with Netsai, but did not have the courage to say it right away.

Netsai bade farewell to *Va*Gwaku, and walked out of his office. She found herself face-to-face with the secretary again, but the secretary's eyes quickly dodged Netsai's gaze. However, Netsai's eyes became fixed at a young lady who was also at the reception talking to the secretary. She was wondering where she had seen the young woman before. Rudo smiled at her and greeted her with the same sweet and innocent voice she had used all those years ago when they had seen each other every day when Netsai and her family were still living in Glen View.

"How are you, aunty?"

"Oh, my, it's you Rudo! You look so big, child. What are you doing here?" Netsai hugged Rudo.

"I work in this building, aunty, so I have come to the reception to pick my boss's letters."

"What kind of job are you doing, Rudo?"

"I am a secretary and our offices are on the fourth floor. My boss runs an accounting firm," Rudo said, still smiling at Netsai.

"How is your mother, Rudo?"

"She is fine."

"Can you pass my regards to her? I am going now," Netsai hurried off.

VaGwaku's secretary was typing some documents on her typewriter while Netsai and Rudo were talking. She made it obvious to Netsai that she did not care about her. Rudo saw that there was tension between the two.

"Why were you ignoring my aunt?" Rudo asked Sarah, the secretary.

"You know what, Rudo? Your aunt is a very stupid woman. When she bought two houses through our agents, I advised her not to let her husband register the houses as a sole owner. She was rude and acted as if I was intruding in her private affairs. She thought I wanted to destroy her marriage. Imagine that! How could I destroy her marriage by simply advising her to have the houses registered in joint ownership? It wasn't my name I wanted on the deeds, but hers," Sarah was still angry with Netsai.

"It wasn't fair for her to say that...,"

"And you know what? Yesterday my boss, VaGwaku, told me that her husband was here. He is planning to register his second wife on one of the houses. The new wife has given birth to twins; imagine how foolish your aunt was."

"Are you serious, Sarah? You know my mum was saying that her husband is the one who collects money from the tenants now! I feel sorry for her, honestly."

It is difficult to advise people like her. She has such a bad attitude," Sarah screwed her face in annoyance.

"Ah, my friend, I beg you to help her. She is my aunt and a very nice person. I don't know what was wrong with her when she was rude with you, but believe me, she is a kind person," Rudo begged her friend to help Netsai. "I will talk to you later about this matter, Sarah, if you don't mind," Rudo said as she walked away from the reception with the mail she had come to collect for her boss.

Herbert collected Aida, who had now been discharged from the hospital, and took her home where she was received by her mother and mother-in-law with a welcome party. They had killed a goat, a cockerel and were thus especially prepared for the new mother. There was a lot of dancing and drinking and both grandmothers gave a name to each child. Aida's mother named one twin Rugare, which means living comfortably, while Herbert's mother named the other, Takunda, which means we have conquered. The names spoke volumes and reflected what either grandmother saw from Herbert and Aida's union. *Va*Soda's choice of name seemed to send a strong message to Netsai, that she had lost Herbert while *Va*Soda and Aida had conquered. For Aida's mother, she was celebrating and reflecting on her daughter's new found wealth.

That night, the party ended late and they woke up very late the following morning. Aida had to wake Herbert to remind him to go to work. Herbert was so excited with the birth of Rugare and Takunda that anyone who did not know Netsai and her children would have thought that those were his first children. Every day was a party for the rest of the week.

As soon as Aida felt strong enough, the lovers went to see *Va*Gwaku to have Aida's name added onto the title deeds of the Milton Park house. When they got to the reception, they were greeted by Sarah. Sarah and Rudo had become very good friends and spent most of the time together chatting during the short breaks. Rudo, who saw Herbert before he saw her, quickly hid her face by burying it in a book she was pretending to read. Herbert did not recognize her. Soon, Herbert and Aida were ushered into *Va*Gwaku's office and Rudo resumed her conversation with Sarah. They were almost whispering.

"*Shaz*, I can't believe this. I nearly choked when I saw them," she said.

"You think he would recognize you? I don't think so," Sarah was alluding to the book reading disguise and laughing. "Even the wife could not remember you when she came last week, so I don't think her husband would remember you."

"You never know my dear friend. Either way, it's better to be cautious than to take a risk," Rudo replied. "When I told my mother about it all, she could not believe it. They were such an admirable and loving couple when they lived on the same street with us. I feel sorry for Netsai. Please, help her," Rudo begged Sarah again.

"Your aunt is too proud. When I gave her advice, I did so because I had seen it happen to my own mother. My mum lost her house to another woman because her name wasn't on the title deeds. I did not want your aunt to go through the same heartbreaking ordeal as my mother."

"Then if that is the case, you should bury the hatchet and help her. You should see it from a feminist point of view. We should fight hard to correct these male domineering tendencies. In that way, we will not only be gaining victory for her, but for all women because she will go around advising other women not to fall into the same pit as she did," Rudo begged. "You never know, maybe tomorrow she will help you as well."

Sarah laughed.

"You know why I laugh? It's because I have heard this kind of talk so many times before. The idea that you help someone so that they may help you as well tomorrow does not ring true with me. I have helped many people who ended up kicking me in the face. Anyway, I will help her because you are my friend. You know my boss ordered Mr Kudzingwa's files from the Deeds Office? We have them in this office, and anytime soon, that woman's name can be registered on the title deeds," Sarah was now whispering into Rudo's ears.

She did not want her boss to overhear their conversation.

"Oh my God! Please do something quickly," Rudo said, covering her mouth with her hand.

"The files are here. Anyway, I don't feel comfortable talking about this issue here at the reception. We can talk about it during our lunch break."

"I will come and collect you for lunch at one pm sharp. We can then talk over lunch," Rudo suggested and Sarah agreed.

Rudo returned to her office feeling sorry for Netsai. The remaining hours of the morning passed in a daze for her. She knew that she had to help Netsai.

CHAPTER Fifteen

Netsai went back to see Lawyer Rusero the following day as per their agreement. But the look on her lawyer's face told her that all was not well; that things were probably not going their way.

"Mrs Kudzingwa, my contact at the Deeds Office said they can not locate the files for the three houses owned by your husband," the lawyer said. Netsai's face went pale. The colour drained from her skin.

"What is even more puzzling the people at the Deeds Office is that there is no record in their office that anyone requested for the files. So whoever took them out of the office did so unlawfully. They have checked everywhere, but the files are definitely not in the office," Ms Rusere said.

Netsai was confused.

"I will phone again while you are here so that you can hear the conversation for yourself." The lawyer instructed her receptionist to connect her with the Deeds Office again.

"Did you by any chance tell anyone that you were planning to have your name registered on the title deeds? It's possible that someone might have told your husband...." before she finished what she wanted to say, the phone rang and her receptionist told her that Mr Chinotimba was on the line.

"I have checked the office again and we can't find those files. I am suspecting that someone took them from this office. Maybe something illegal is going on," Mr Chinotimba said. The phone was put on speaker, so that Netsai could hear everything.

"If you don't find them by the end of the day, I think it is best to inform the Police Criminal Investigations Department," Nancy Rusere suggested.

"My team leader also made the same remark. We just have to wait and see," Mr Chinotimba said.

"I will check with you again tomorrow, thank you very much Mr Chinotimba. Bye!"

"Bye!"

"I am sorry we can't do much today, Mrs Kudzingwa. I suggest you go back home and wait to hear from me. Please don't say anything to anyone, in case your husband is alerted if he is involved in the disappearance of the files."

"I will not do anything to jeopardise the case," Netsai replied.

She was visibly shaken by the whole issue of the disappearing files just when she thought she was correcting her past mistakes.

"I can't believe that something like this is happening to me. What wrong have I done to deserve this misfortune? Please do whatever best you can to help me, Ms Rusero," Netsai begged. She was shedding tears.

"Don't worry Mrs Kudzingwa. If he is responsible for the disappearance of the files, he shall not get away with it. The law is there to prosecute criminals like him and protect innocent citizens like you," Nancy said, seeing Netsai to the door.

After Netsai left, Nancy began to talk to herself. "I think it's high time women woke up and realised that buying houses with a husband should be treated just like any other business. Why are women so naïve? Love is something that can fade and disappear at any time. Maybe we need to start publishing fliers and posters to educate women on proprietary rights!" she said as she sat in her big, leather reclining chair. "Honestly, I can not work so hard and then have some woman come and claim what belongs to me and make it hers!" she shook her head.

When Netsai arrived home, she was surprised to find Rudo waiting for her. From her appearance and facial features, it was clear that there was something bothering her.

"Ah, Rudo? You have decided to come and see me at my new house today, after all these years," Netsai said embracing Rudo. For a moment she forgot about the missing files.

"Aunty, I am not staying for a long time. Can you walk me to the gate because I want to say something to you in private?" Rudo said, rising from the chair and getting ready to leave.

"It's okay, we can walk to the gate," Netsai said.

"Where is your husband?" Rudo asked as they stepped outside. Netsai knew that whatever Rudo wanted to say, and which made her so nervous, was something very important.

"He is not here. Is everything alright, Rudo?"

"Yes, aunty, everything is ok, let's walk a bit further away from here. I can't say much now," Rudo said, increasing her pace. Netsai was almost trotting to keep up.

"What is it Rudo? I am now getting more and more anxious?" Netsai asked.

"I don't want your husband to come and find me here. In fact, he should not even get to know that I came to see you," Rudo said.

"Ah, if that is the case, I think we are much better off inside the house, in the girls' bedroom. Outside the gate, he can pull up any time from any direction. He will even be more suspicious to see us talking outside the gate. Inside my house I can say you are a customer who came to have her measurements taken. Many people come here to try their dresses or to be measured for size. Let's go back inside, my dear child."

Netsai was a bit more settled now. They walked back into the house and went to the girls' bedroom. In the bedroom Rudo pulled out three files from her bag, and handed them to Netsai. They were the title deeds.

"Aunty, this is a very dangerous thing I am doing and either myself or my friend, or both of us, can lose our jobs if this gets to Mr Gwaku's ears. My friend, Sarah, the receptionist with whom you had a misunderstanding when you bought your houses, gave me these papers. She is the one who gave me your address because we thought you needed our help," Rudo said.

Netsai cried with happiness. "Rudo, my child, you are my saviour, my angel. What would I have done without you?"

"Aunty, it was not easy to get these documents from my friend, I had to persuade her to give me the files. "

"I do understand, Rudo. After the way I treated her when we bought these houses, she has every reason to be angry with me," Netsai said, tears streaming down her cheeks. "That day when I saw you chatting with her, I was embarrassed and it took a lot of courage for me to walk into that office," Netsai said, tears of joy flooding her cheeks.

"She told me everything that happened, but I told her that you are a really nice person," Rudo said.

"Thank you very much, Rudo. I was coming from my lawyer when I found you there because after my husband married the other woman, I was advised by my friend to safeguard my proprietary rights by registering my names on all our three houses. And now the Deeds Office was telling my lawyer that they could not locate the files."

Netsai explained everything to Rudo, who also told Netsai that Aida and Herbert had been to the office that day in connection with registering Aida's name on the title deeds. Netsai could not believe her luck, which had come at the eleventh hour. "Let this be a lesson to you Rudo when you get married. You must always remember that love can fade and you should be very cautious when it comes to buying property with a man."

"I was discussing your ordeal with my mum last night and she is really angry about the whole thing. She was telling me the same thing, about being careful when getting into relationships. It's so bad, you know, what Uncle Herbert is doing to you," said Rudo.

"You know what? God answered my prayers at the last minute. Firstly I saw my friend, who advised me to get a lawyer's advice about registering my name on the houses. I went to see the lawyer only two days ago, and I walked into *Va*Gwaku's office and saw you talking to Sarah, and today you saved me by rescuing these files before Herbert tempered with the title deeds .God is great and he works in a mysterious way," Netsai was very happy. "The way *Va*Gwaku was avoiding my eyes when I saw him alerted me that there was something he was hiding from me. I don't know how to thank you, my child," Netsai was looking at the files because she wanted to be sure that they were indeed the original documents.

"It's okay, aunty. We all need to help one another in times like these. I think I have to go now, it is getting late." Rudo said. "Should I leave these documents here with you? Do you think they will be safe?"

"I am not sure. Herbert can see them and I will lose the whole case," Netsai said, trying to figure out how to keep the documents safe. She did not want anything to go wrong.

"I think I will go with them tonight and tomorrow morning I will take them to your lawyer's office," Rudo suggested. "Or we can meet tomorrow at 8 o'clock in the morning outside your lawyer's office. I will pass on the documents to you then."

"I think that is a very brilliant idea. The lawyer had asked me to go and see her in the afternoon, but I can always see her in the morning because she too, was very worried about these documents." Netsai handed Rudo the files, who put them in her handbag and bade Netsai farewell."

"Can't you wait for something to eat, Rudo? A cup of tea or a drink?" Netsai asked Rudo.

"No, aunty, not today. I now know where you live. I will visit you some other time when all this is over, and then we can have lots of food to eat and cool drinks. I want to get home early and do other things," Rudo said, leaving the room. Netsai walked her to the gate, and on the way, they saw Herbert's car coming. They were on the driveway and Rudo greeted Herbert, who did not seem to recognize her.

"Have you forgotten her? That's Rudo, Luke's sister. You know the guy who used to carry my things to the buyers when I began the business?" Netsai reminded Herbert.

"Ah! I had forgotten her. She is now a big girl, a young woman in fact. How are you Rudo? Times move very fast," Herbert said as he exchanged handshakes with Rudo. "Of course, I remember Luke very well, *Amai*Farai. They only lived a few houses from us. And how is your brother Luke doing? I haven't seen him for ages."

"I am fine, uncle, if you are well too," Rudo said, shaking Herbert's hand. "Luke is fine. He is now married and has two children."

"Send my regards to him."

"Rudo is just leaving," Netsai told Herbert. "You can go now Rudo. I shall not waste any more of your time. Let me see to *Babava*Farai. Go well, my child," Netsai said to Rudo.

"You see, I am very selfish. I am going in her direction. I could have given her a lift," Herbert said after Rudo had already left.

"Maybe she isn't going home straight away," Netsai wanted to discourage Herbert from offering Rudo a lift, because of the files she was carrying in her bag. She did not want anything to go wrong.

Rudo walked very fast until she reached the shops where she got a kombi to town, where she would have to catch another one to get home. Herbert went into the house where he sat down and started watching television. Netsai went to her sewing room and Herbert followed her. Netsai was so preoccupied she did not see Herbert standing at the door.

"These days you really don't care about me any more. You can't tell me that I am now invisible. You can't even see that I am standing by the door?"

"Sorry, I am very busy I did not realize you followed me into the sewing room. Very sorry," Netsai was surprised to see Herbert standing by the door.

"What kind of a life is this, when your family ignores you, both your wife and children?" Herbert asked.

"I am very busy, *Babava*Farai. If I don't finish this dress tonight, I will not have money to buy food for the children," Netsai answered, still concentrating on her sewing.

"You are always complaining about the shortage of money. If you are not careful, I will ban this sewing business on my property," Herbert wanted to pick a quarrel with Netsai. But she just shook her head and continued sewing. "I can chase you from my house, forever! Do you hear me? And the way your children behave towards me, I now doubt if they are really my children. My mother was right, when she said that you used me as a jacket father for other men's children. Now it's written all over their faces. You did not tell me about Farai's scholarship. When I come here , that boy doesn't give a damn about respecting me. He doesn't even get up to greet me. It is now evident that he is not my child."

Netsai did not say anything. Herbert stormed out of the room and went to the lounge where he collected his car keys and left.

Netsai was left tongue-tied. She blamed her old-fashioned parents for not allowing her to divorce Herbert. She put her sewing work aside and sat on the chair till she fell asleep.

Herbert went to Milton Park where he found Aida breastfeeding one of the boys. He picked the other one up and put the baby on his lap.

"You are my only children, my true biological children. I doubt their paternity my children in Eastlea," he said. Tears began to roll down his cheeks.

"What is it, darling? What makes you sad and to cry like this?" Aida asked. "*Amai*, come and see, your son is upset and is crying! I don't know what the problem is," Aida called out to *Va*Soda

"What is it, my son? What is it *Mufakose*?" His mother addressed him by his totem, as she tightened the wrapper she had round her waist.

"*Amai*, I don't think those children in Eastlea are really mine. You know when you told me that they don't look like they are my biological children, I did not believe you. But now I understand it. Farai, Tariro and Rutendo are not my children. I was used by that woman as a jacket cover," Herbert said, tears rolling down his cheeks. "I am going to chase that woman out of my house, together with her children," he said, shaking his head, looking aggrieved.

"It's alright, my son. There is no need for you to trouble your soul like this, *Mufakose*. You think the ancestors who opened Aida's womb and gave you twin boys did not know what they were doing? They knew you had been used by that whore, and now they have given you two healthy baby boys. What more do you want?"

Herbert placed the child he was holding on the sofa and began to pace the lounge. He was very angry.

"That woman does not know me very well. What kind of a woman is she? Umm? I have been feeding her, giving her everything and now this is how she repays me?"

"She has a bad omen, a bad spirit that does not want her to live in luxury. Stupid woman!" *Va*Soda added. Herbert went to bed. Aida offered him some food, but he refused. *Va*Soda and Aida remained in the lounge for some time. Aida had never seen Herbert cry and was deeply disturbed.

The following morning Herbert went to *Va*Gwaku's office, where he was told that his title deeds files were missing. Herbert was angry with *Va*Gwaku whom he thought was playing games with him.

"*Mudhara*, you take me for a fool? I want those title deeds here and now! How can you tell me this rubbish that the files can not be located and yet the person who came to collect the files from your office came from the Deeds Office?"

"Let me call my secretary, who can explain to you what the person who came to collect them looked like," *Va*Gwaku was now scared because of Herbert's outburst. He called Sarah into the office.

"Sarah, can you please tell Mr Kudzingwa about the person who came here to collect those files, please," he asked his secretary.

"Let me check in the visitor's book to see his name," Sarah said, going to the front desk to collect the visitor's book. "Here, this is where the person signed. That is his name and signature," Sarah said handing *Va*Gwaku the visitor's register.

"Let me check with the guy who brought these files here to see if he can identify this name," *Va*Gwaku suggested. He dialled the number for his contact at the Deeds Office, the person who had smuggled the files out of the same office. He was shaking his head as he talked to his contact on the phone. Herbert was now getting more agitated with each passing minute. *Va*Gwaku finished talking to the person on the phone and began to fidget with the pen in his hand. Herbert looked at him with a piercing gaze.

"The Deeds Office said they have two office orderlies, and one of them did not come to work today. It's possible that he misfiled them, so they will talk to him tomorrow when he returns to work. They think he could be the one who came to retrieve them from our office. " he explained.

"*Mudhara*, I don't want my plans to be ruined. You are now confusing me. Today you tell me the files are here, tomorrow you tell me someone took them back to the Deeds Office, and the following day you tell me no one can locate them? I was planning to bring Aida here tomorrow to finalize everything, and now this!"

"You can still sign the deed-of-sale forms tomorrow when you bring her. That won't be a problem," *Va*Gwaku said trying to pacify Herbert.

"I will hear what Aida says, but I don't really want to disappoint her," Herbert said, as a matter-of-fact. Why would they need them? He had not hinted to Netsai what he intended to do with the Milton Park and Glen View houses.

"You worry too much, *Munin'ina*. Leave it to me," *Va*Gwaku said trying to regain the confidence of his client. "It is probably a mix-up."

* * *

Netsai was at Lawyer Nancy Rusero's office with the bundle of files in her hand. She begged the receptionist to let her see the lawyer as soon as she could. When she got into the office, Nancy was surprised to see her client so early and holding some files. Netsai was all smiles.

"I thought we were meant to meet this afternoon, Mrs Kudzingwa?" Nancy asked.

"Afternoon was going to be too late. I won't take much of your time, a few minutes will be enough," Netsai said, apologetically.

"Anyway, my first client comes in at 8.30 am so we have fifteen minutes to talk about whatever you want to tell me," Nancy said, giving Netsai a seat. Netsai handed the lawyer the three files. Nancy was surprised to see the files with Herbert's title deeds.

"Aren't these the files we were looking for? Where did you find them?"

Netsai laughed before telling Nancy the whole story.

"Thank you very much, Mrs Kudzingwa. I think you are a very lucky woman. Let me make an application to the Deeds Office straightaway, so that they put on hold any other applications regarding these houses. I will fax the application to them today, and send the original letters by post. We need to move very fast," Nancy said. She took her note book and drafted a letter addressed to the Deeds Office and gave it to her secretary to type and fax to the Deeds Office.

"By the end of the month everything will be sorted. Your husband won't be able to sell or transfer these houses into anyone's name without your consent and agreement," Nancy assured Netsai, who left the office feeling like a small girl who had just received a doll from her mother. To think that the day before she had left the same office in tears was utterly unbelievable. Nancy decided to take the application to the Deed Office in person because she now knew that there was someone working in the same office who had stolen the files and delivered them to Mr. Gwaku, and the fax would most likely have fallen into the wrong hands. She was a very good lawyer who wanted to satisfy her clients.

Herbert decided to give *Va*Gwaku a few days to retrieve the files. After a week, he decided to go back to *Va*Gwaku's office to see if the files had been found and brought back. *Va*Gwaku was not in the office. He returned to work very angry. He tried phoning *Va*Gwaku and each time Sarah picked the phone, she gave him different excuses. Trying to call *Va*Gwaku's direct number was also fruitless. There were no cell-phones in those days. Herbert had two options; either to go through Sarah, the receptionist, or phone using a direct line. When he eventually got hold of him on the phone, *Va*Gwaku told him that he had a family emergency to attend to.

"So can I see you after work?" Herbert asked. He was now desperate.

"It won't be possible because my wife is coming to pick me up anytime from around three in the afternoon to take me to the hospital to see my nephew, so you won't find me here," *Va*Gwaku said. He had found out that Netsai's lawyer had applied for her name to be included on the title deeds, and the High Court had issued an injunction order barring Herbert from selling the house or adding his second wife's name on any of the houses. Netsai's name was added on the three houses successfully. *Va*Gwaku had accepted bribery from Herbert to do the job unlawfully; through the back door, and now he did not know how to break the news to Herbert. VaGwaku managed to dodge Herbert for another week.

Herbert suspected something was wrong, and asked someone else to call *Va*Gwaku's number. The secretary, who had answered the phone, not expecting Herbert on the other end, handed the phone to *Va*Gwaku

"Oh, it's you, *Munin'ina*? Can you come and see me in the afternoon if you can?" he said, after he realised that Herbert had set him up. When Herbert arrived at the office, *Va*Gwaku dialled the Deeds Office and quietly handed the phone to Herbert.

"Hallo, your estate agent phoned this office today requesting the files with your title deeds. The title deeds were in the hands of your wife's lawyer when he was looking for them. Your wife's lawyer has successfully applied to register your wife on all the three properties. So you no longer own the three properties as a sole owner, but in joint ownership with Mrs Netsai Kudzingwa..."

Herbert's face went grey. He was in shock. VaGwaku looked at him, waiting for him to say something, but he said nothing. He kept holding the receiver in his hand, which VaGwaku took from his hand and placed down.

"You heard it yourself. Your wife acted first. All the time we were looking for the files, they were at her lawyer's office," he said

"So you were avoiding me because you knew all along? You made me appear stupid, phoning you everyday, and instead of telling me the truth, you decided to waste my time?" Herbert looked at *Va*Gwaku with blood-shot eyes.

"Leave me out of your mess, young man. I know nothing beyond what you know," *Va*Gwaku said. He just wanted Herbert to leave his office.

"You think I am foolish? You were playing hide-and-seek with me!" Herbert was now shouting. "I want my money back, now!"

"What is it, Mr Gwaku? Should I call in the security guards?" Sarah asked.

"Don't worry about me, I will go and sort this out with my wife," Herbert said, when he realised that he could end up being escorted from the premises by security guards. He pushed Sarah to one side as he stormed out of the office.

"Behave yourself, you foolish man. What gives you the power to push me towards the wall like that? You have never been disciplined by women, isn't it? I will beat you up until your trousers falls to your knees, if you don't know me very well!" Sarah was angry. She shouted at Herbert as she struggled to regain her balance.

"Just clear out of the way!" Herbert shouted back.

"Herbert, I was respecting you like a man all along. What gives you the right to harass my staff like this? You think you are the only person who can get angry? Leave my premises respectfully," *Va*Gwaku said, his hands in his pockets. Within a few seconds, most of the staff from adjacent offices had gathered at *Va*Gwaku's office to see what was causing the commotion.

"What is it, Mr Gwaku?" one young man asked.

"It's that silly beggar who lives off his wife's pockets!" *Va*Gwaku replied, pointing at Herbert. Herbert realised that he maybe manhandled by the group of people who had gathered in the foyer. He remembered what had happened to him when he had been assaulted by Tendai and his friends on the day he had given Netsai the divorce token. He got into his car and drove to Eastlea, to deal with Netsai.

When he got into the house, Netsai was on her sewing machine. Herbert pulled the plug out of the socket.

"What is it, Herbert?" Netsai asked.

"You don't know what it is? You bitch, whore!" Herbert was ready for a fight

"You just come here moody and expect me to know what it is that is bothering you? If you are fed up with me and my children and our house, please, don't come here!" Netsai shouted back.

"Now you are a little queen, who can rule me, isn't it? Is that why you registered your name on my houses without my permission?"

"Our houses! They were never your houses alone, Herbert. Those houses belong to you and me and our children, Farai, Tariro and Rutendo. If you want a house for your wife, go and work hard as I did and buy her a house. I am not bothered. You can't take what belongs to me and give it to another woman. It's just not fair!" Netsai did not care anymore.

"I will teach you a lesson today. Where have you ever seen a married woman owning a house?"

"But Aida, your second wife, is the only woman who can own a house?"

"Yes, she deserves all the houses because she bore me two boys at the same time, twins!"

"You can give her what you work for together, not the product of my sweat! Over my dead body!"

"Instead of begging for forgiveness, you are bragging about it!" Herbert slapped Netsai in the face and began to assault her in earnest. Tsitsi, upon hearing the commotion, ran to the sewing room, but could not open the door. It was locked from inside. She rushed outside and asked the tenants at the backyard quarters for help. The boys who occupied the quarters came and pushed the door open and stormed in.

Herbert could have killed Netsai had the guys not kicked the door open. She had been brutalised more than he had ever done before. He was revenging the embarrassment he had suffered at *Va*Gwaku's office. Netsai had to be admitted into hospital, where she spent the night.

* * *

Netsai went to see her aunt in Mufakose as soon as she was discharged from the hospital. Seeing the state she was in, *Tete* Susan went to see her parents in order to inform them about Netsai's latest ordeal. She came back to her house followed by her brother and Netsai's mother.

Netsai's mother was shocked by Herbert's brutality. *Atete*, what is all this?" she asked.

"That is why I have called you. To me, it is obvious that Herbert does not want Netsai any more. He nearly killed her, and it's now up to you, her mother who carried her for nine months in your womb, to rescue her...,"

"Did you find out why he assaulted her because I don't think he would just assault her for no reason at all," Netsai's father asked.

"*Baba* is right. We need to know why they fought before we take sides.

"Can't you see that your daughter's life is in danger?"

"*Atete,* we are all married. A woman has to respect her husband otherwise her husband can beat her if she doesn't zip her mouth."

"Ah-ya-a," *Tete*Susan sighed. "Netsai, your parents want to know why you fought," she addressed her niece, who was lying on the sofa. *Tete*Susan could not believe that even if Netsai had provoked Herbert, she would deserve to be brutalised to that extent, or at all.

"He assaulted me because I registered my name on all the three houses. He wanted to give one of the houses to his new wife. So I went to a lawyer and she registered my name on the title deeds," Netsai explained.

"What is a title deeds?" her mother asked.

Her father knew what title deeds were, but wanted Netsai to explain.

"It's a legal document which shows ownership of a property. All along our houses were in Herbert's name alone, now we own all of them together."

"Did you ask for permission before you did that?" her father asked.

"I did that to safeguard my interests because I did not want his second wife to enjoy the fruits of my labour," Netsai explained, crying.

"Even if he had put another wife's name on the title deeds, what would have been the problem? He wasn't going to make you homeless. You have one of the houses so I don't see your problem," Netsai's mother said. "You are very jealous Netsai, and nothing more."

"Where is your husband now, Netsai?" *Tete* Susan asked. She did not know what else to say. All she knew was that if Netsai were her daughter, she would not allow Herbert to lay a finger on her again.

"He is in police custody," Netsai replied.

"You had to go all the way to the police?" *Tete* Susan asked, shocked at the mention of police.

"If I let him off the hook, *Tete*, that man will kill me. Let the law take its course," Netsai replied.

"This is something else," Netsai's mother shook her head.

"My sister, you have a big job here, to make Netsai mend her ways. My daughter is behaving like a man and there is only one rooster in every homestead. If you keep two roosters under the same roof, they fight until one is killed. My daughter thinks she is a man. Now she has reported her husband to the police. Why involve the police? You are foolish, Netsai. I don't want you in my house. You deserve the beatings. I would also have done the same if your mother went to a lawyer to put her name on my house and I would divorce her if she took me to the police. You are not married to the police, you should know that!" Netsai's father was fuming.

"I am concerned about my daughter involving the police in this domestic matter. Which house do you know has been made to stand firm due to police intervention? That's no respect for a man who paid *lobola* for you," her mother said. "What do you think his relatives will say when they hear that their son has been arrested?"

"I don't keep rubbish in my house. You want to follow your aunt Bessie's footsteps, who thinks that the car she drives is her husband? From here, you have nowhere to go," her father said, leaving *Tete* Susan's house. As an after thought, he turned to his wife and said, "You stay here, with your sister-in-law, and plan what you are going to do with her, but do not bring her to my house, you hear me?"

"Yes, *Baba*, I hear you," Netsai's mother replied.

Netsai did not say anything, neither did her aunt. After her father left, her mother began to talk.

"You have heard the words from your father's mouth. Now you are dragging me into all this mess you created yourself because of title deeds. Have you seen my name on any title deeds? You know your father very well. I can not even go home with him now because he thinks I did not raise you well."

"This is a very complicated issue, *muroora....*"

"*Vatete*, we are both married. What is wrong to leave the house registered in one's husband's name? Who told her to fiddle with that? She thinks she is a man? She listens to gossip too much."

"It wasn't gossip mother, but it was something real. Herbert was planning to give one of the houses to his new wife," Netsai explained again. "I will never allow another woman to benefit from my hard work."

"*Muroora*, we are only women in this house at the moment, let's be honest with one another. There is nothing wrong with what Netsai did. Who wants to work for another woman? We all know how hardworking Netsai is, how she spent sleepless nights sewing dresses. sometimes using candle-light. I would not allow my husband to do that and I don't think you would allow my brother to do that to you, either," *Tete* Susan was trying to put some sense into Netsai's mother, who she knew was too scared of her husband to think logically, in case she made him angry.

"I don't know what to say or do, *Vatete*. All I can do is to leave her in your care. You take her back to her husband's house. It's your duty to train her how to look after a husband well. Netsai, my daughter, I am going back home to your father. A man is the head of the family. You just accept whatever he wants to do. You listen too much to this feminist talk," she said as she rose to leave.

*Tete*Susan escorted Netsai's mother and on the way she pleaded with her sister-in-law to feel the pain of the mother who gave birth to Netsai, and try to understand her daughter's predicament. But Netsai's mother would not have any of it. She said that as a church leader, her duty was to see that Netsai remained married, and was submissive to her husband's needs and demands.

CHAPTER Sixteen

Aida paid Herbert's bail and he was released soon afterwards. *Tete* Susan begged her niece to drop the charges against Herbert, and against her will, she did so. Herbert's case was dropped. That did not stop Herbert from harbouring a grudge against Netsai, however.

Soon after his release, Herbert visited his brother, Lameck, to spread propaganda against his wife. He found his brother polishing his shoes; he was sitting on the veranda of his house.

"*Mukoma*, I have come to tell you about how evil that woman is. Can you imagine your own wife, *Amai*Rujeko, taking you to the police after a domestic dispute?"

"Who was reported to the police?" Lameck asked, not paying particular attention to Herbert as he continued applying polish to his shoes.

"I was in police cells for nearly three days, imagine! She called the police when we fought at our house," Herbert was shaking his head to emphasise his point.

"What had made you fight?" Lameck asked, examining his shoes.

"*Amai*Farai has no respect for me. Imagine she went to see a lawyer to add her name on our houses, my houses, without my permission. Now her name appears on all title deeds."

"At least your wife can stand up for her rights. This is good news. Isn't she now a very clever woman? Umm, someone who can stand up to bullying and domestic violence! I am proud of her," Lameck was laughing as he said this, putting his polished shoes on his feet.

"*Mukoma*, why do you support the woman? I only came to have a brotherly chat with you, and you laugh at me and treat me like a fool?" Herbert was getting angry.

"Herbert, don't waste my time with your chat. First of all, you did not fight with your wife, but you hit her and she did not retaliate. You nearly killed her. That's domestic violence. She did the right thing to take you to the police. Secondly, all your assumed problems are of your own making. You sort them out yourself, and please don't involve me. You said that yourself when I called you to meet so that l could give you advice; have you forgotten that? You made your bed, now lie in it." Lameck was angry with Herbert. Herbert realised that his brother was in no mood to feel sorry for him, and he left the veranda quietly without saying good bye. He felt humiliated.

"Go, you idiot of a brother!" Lameck shouted after him.

"Your brother is losing his sanity. Whatever that Aida gave him, it's something terrible," *Amai*Rujeko said, both hands resting on her waist.

She had been within earshot when Herbert was talking to Lameck, but did not want to interfere because in the Shona culture, when one sees two brothers fighting, it is wise to keep one's distance. Blood is thicker than water.

"He is mad, and I am so happy that *Amai*Farai reported him to the police, and registered her name on the title deeds. Shameless man!" *Amai*Rujeko added, and hissed through her teeth.

"Well, he is tasting his own medicine. They say a mad man who refuses to take medicine cannot be rid of his illness. He will learn the hard way. He wants to practice polygamy using resources earned by another woman and expects peace to reign?"

Meanwhile, *Va*Soda, Herbert's mother, feeling enraged by her son's arrest, decided to take the matter into her own hands and execute justice on behalf of her son. She took her small wrapper which she threw on her shoulder and armed with her walking stick; boarded a bus and went to Lameck to garner the support of her eldest son before going to Netsai's parent's house.

"*Amai*, instead of apologising to *Amai*Farai's family and *Amai*Farai herself for the brutality of your son, are you not embarrassed to come here and accuse her of reporting your son to the police? You are urging your son to brutalise his wife by turning a blind eye to the brutality. If Herbert gets into deeper problems, you have no one but yourself to blame," Lameck said as a matter of fact.

"How can you say that to me, Lameck? How would you feel if your son was put in police custody by a woman he looks after and feeds like a broiler chicken?"

"Hoo, you now see *Amai*Farai as the benefactor of your son's wealth? Is it not *Amai*Farai who is the breadwinner of that family? You treat Herbert with kid's gloves. He needs reproaching and not sympathy," Lameck said. "If Herbert wants to be a polygamist, he should do it the right way. He never informed me that he was marrying another woman. Yet you knew, and you shielded him and encouraged him. You are two-faced, *Amai*, and one day you will find yourself at the receiving end. I have nothing further to say to you, but that you need to correct your son where he is doing wrong instead of encouraging him; call a spade a spade. Now if you will excuse me, I have work to do."

Lameck and his mother had a thorny relationship because he always told her facts when- ever he thought she was in the wrong. He refused to divorce his wife whom his mother did not like. If he had followed her advice, he would have ended up like Herbert. His mother had not forgiven him for openly being on the side of his wife whenever she complained about *Amai*Rujeko. Realising that she wasn't heading anywhere with Lameck, she boarded a bus to Marimba in Mufakose, to Netsai's parents.

* * *

Joyce Jenje-Makwenda

"I have come here to give you a piece of my mind. I respected you as a family into which my son married, but my respect is now weaning away because of your daughter's behaviour. How dare she take my son to jail? My son bought your daughter a house and a car, and she shows her gratitude by taking him to the police? This is the second time she has taken my son to the police. What wrong has he done to deserve this treatment?"

*Va*Soda went on and on about how and what Herbert had done for ungrateful. She did not give Netsai's mother any chance to respond, until when she felt that she had said all she wanted to say. She then sighed and began to cry.

"Ah, *vamukurungayi*, my in-law, I don't really know what is wrong with our daughter. Whatever has gotten into her head is bringing this family into disrepute. Imagine, I am a leader at my church, I preach good morals every Sunday, but my own daughter turns out to be like this. I am very worried, especially about her reporting *Babava*Farai to the police. I am sorry."

While she was talking, Samuel, Netsai's brother, came into the house. They had not see him come into the house because he had used the back door. "You know, I am yet to see any other woman in this town who has been so lucky as to have a husband like Herbert. My son was taking your daughter to places we never went to, holidaying and enjoying themselves, and what did he get in return? Your daughter turned herself into a cruel woman and now she wants to run my son's affairs," *Va*Soda took an envelope in which she kept a photo and displayed it on the table. That was the same photo she had taken from Netsai's photo album. Netsai's mother looked at the photo and could not believe her eyes. Her father, who was also in the lounge, looked at the photo as well and shook his head in embarrassment.

"Your daughter is very spoilt. What else does she want in life? A husband who gives you everything, money, houses and a car and she thanks him by parading her naked body at beaches...." Samuel could not take the abuse of his sister anymore.

"What kind of good life are you talking about, you shameless old witch? And you two, who are supposed to defend your daughter who is being slowly murdered by this brute called Herbert," he was pointing his index finger at his mother and father, "sit and listen to this gibberish from a shameless old woman, whose son is brutalising your own child." He pointed at *Va*Soda. "Old woman, what do you mean when you say my sister is living in luxury, what kind of luxury? Is brutality luxury? Did Netsai not pay most of the money for those houses and the cars you are talking about? Your son is only a driver, and where have you seen people earning peanuts like him buying three houses and two cars? Is that not my sister's money, my sister who spent sleepless nights threading needles and prickling her fingers in candle-lit darkness, sewing clothes to sell? Your son thanks our daughter by humiliating her, marrying a well-known prostitute. Get out of this house now, before I smack your old and smelling arse!" Samuel was pocking the old woman in the face. "And how dare you parade my sister's photograph, you witch? When did you steal the photo from her? If your idiot of a son is fed up with my sister, I am here to take care of her. I can take her back, and those houses are rightfully hers so you better get used to the idea now." Samuel was known for speaking his mind and his short-temper.

"My son, control your temper. Our in-law here has only come to see if we can fix things between Netsai and her son....!" Samuel's father was cut short by Samuel.

"You have no shame, *Baba*, to sit here and slander your own daughter before this old witch, and you witch, get out of this house before I throw you out," Samuel took the photo which was on the table and grabbed Herbert's mother by the hand. She left the house in a huff, realising that Samuel could do anything to her. She even forgot her walking stick and wrapper, which Samuel threw after her. Netsai's mother followed her in-law to the gate and to the bus stop, all the while begging for forgiveness. *VaSoda* was crying all the way and not saying anything. Netsai's mother returned to the house. She was very angry and wanted to admonish her son.

Samuel was arguing with his father, whom he was accusing of greed and hypocrisy.

"If you keep nagging me, I will go to the bus stop and beat that stupid old woman. You know me very well," he was pacing in the house.

"You are possessed by an evil spirit. How dare you embarrass us before our in-law? You want them to send Netsai away, and for her to come and live here? No ways!" his father said.

"If there is anyone who is possessed by the evil spirit, it's that woman you are defending. How dare she allow her son to brutalise someone else's daughter? Did you not feel any pain bringing Netsai into this world, *Amai?*"

"If he beats her, she is his wife, is there anything wrong with that? Do you think all men are under petticoat government like you? If she wants to copy what your wife does, her husband will discipline her for sure. Your sister is listening to this women's rights gospel too much. Your mother here does not have the women's rights that she is yearning for, yet she is happily married to me," Samuel's father said.

"It depends on what you call a happy marriage. I would never let any man beat my daughter, never ever, if I call myself a man and a father. No man will beat my Ruvimbo, and get away with it! I am going to take Netsai from that idiot and help her get a divorce. I want to see anyone who will come to my house challenging that... As for my wife, leave her out of this..."

"Since when did Netsai become your child, son? Did you give birth to her?" his mother was now angry.

"She is my sister. I have a moral duty to protect her if her own parents can not." Samuel said. He left his parents seated in the room, reeling like wounded beasts.

Meanwhile, Herbert and Aida were having a heated argument. "So all along you were lying to me about giving me one of the houses? You thought I was a fool who could not find out the truth?" Aida was fuming. "Tell me, Herbert, were you sorting things with your wife, and lying to me that you would transfer the house into my name, is that so?"

"No Aida, that's not the case. Can you listen to what I want to say to you, Aida, please?" Herbert reached out to hold Aida's hand, but she pushed him away. She went into the children's bedroom where she began changing her babies' nappies. She changed them into clean clothes. She packed an overnight bag. Herbert was standing in the room, trying to talk to her, but Aida was miming a song playing on the radio, and not paying attention to him. She changed into nice clothes and put one baby in the pram and the other on her back, and secured him with a beach towel. She left the house, still singing.

"Where are you going, Aida?" Herbert asked, trying to block Aida's way.

"Please just get out of my way! Please Herbert!" Aida wriggled her way past, and stormed out of the house.

"Okay, Aida, at least let me take you to wherever you want to go, in the car, please. It's not good to take the babies into the cold like this," Herbert said, fetching his car keys.

"Can you leave me alone, Herbert?" she said, refusing to get into the car. "When you know that I and my babies deserve better, you can come and fetch us. I am not a stupid person to be taken for granted. I don't live in a house registered in another woman's name.

Never!" she said and continued walking to the main road.

Herbert saw his world falling apart. He felt dizzy and started crying. He knew that he would never manage to buy Aida a house even if he wanted to. He couldn't sell the house in Glen View. He couldn't sell any of the houses. His job was not paying him enough money to sustain the life of the businessman he was pretending to be. Netsai had closed her sewing shop in town, where he used to go and take money from the till. The commuter omnibus transport business which Netsai was running was also grounded because he had taken all the money from the drivers, and in the end, Netsai could not afford to maintain the buses let alone pay the drivers and conductors. And to make matter worse, he had accepted money for deposit from a couple he wanted to sell the Glen View house to. Not only that, he had also spent all the money on bribing *Va*Gwaku and showering Aida with presents.

* * *

Samuel went to see *Tete*Susan to tell her that he was taking Netsai to go and live with him at his house. *Tete* Susan was reluctant because she did not want any friction with her brother, but Samuel would not take no for an answer.

"*Tete*, I will take Netsai whether you agree or not. I can not stand by and watch my sister being brutalised by a man who suffers from low self esteem and inferiority complex. I will deal with *Baba* if he comes here to blame you. I have just been to his house, where I have given him a mouthful. I want to deal with Herbert head-on, man-to-man, if he dares to come to my house. The drama that will take place will be in the papers the following day, if he dares."

Netsai did not say anything. She excused herself and went to sleep.

"*Tete*, can't you see that my sister has lost a lot of weight since her monster husband started bashing her? We need to do something to help her. She is not the first person to have a failed marriage. *Baba* is obsessed with a divorce token issued in front of a witness. That is rubbish. Netsai was married in the courts. She did not elope with Herbert, so I don't see why the old man wants her to follow these archaic procedures, which are no longer relevant. She will get a divorce through the courts and she needs our support and not rejection," Samuel was talking like a preacher. His aunt was nodding her head, and tears welled in her eyes but she quickly suppressed them.

"*Tete*, it's time you become firm with your brother and make him do the right thing. Why are you so scared of him?"

*Tete*Susan just laughed. She did not know what to say, but she knew Samuel had a valid point. "You know my nephew; your father has always been a very difficult man. Even with your mother, they used to fight a lot and all the disputes ended up here. I think I can write a best seller novel about my experiences with your parents. Your father probably identifies a lot with Herbert. I just don't know what is wrong with him. I think your father thinks wife beating is normal, and that women bring it on themselves."

"He has a serious problem. But *Tete*, make sure Netsai does not return to that monster. He is damaging her self esteem and confidence," Samuel begged his aunt.

"I agree with you, Netsai needs a break. Your mother doesn't make it easier for her either. She is always on your father's side. Maybe she thinks he can beat her as well, if she goes against his wishes. I don't know."

"*Tete*, whether father and mother fight because of this, I don't care. I am taking Netsai to my house. Anyone who is not happy about it, tell them to come to Borrowdale. They will find me ready for them, especially Herbert. It's time he fights with me if he wants to fight because any man who beats a woman is a coward."

"They will not come there to bother you, I am sure, they will come here. I am glad that you have come to Netsai's rescue."

"If anyone harasses you, let me know and I can deal with them." *Tete* Susan went to wake Netsai up because Samuel was waiting for her, but Netsai said she wanted to sleep a little longer. Samuel decided to go and return in the evening to collect her. Netsai did not want to sleep as she had claimed, but wanted more time to assess the situation. She knew her brother was fond of her, but she also knew that her mother would direct her threats and attacks towards Samuel's wife, blaming her for giving her shelter. That had happened before. Eventually she relented and went to live with Samuel.

Meanwhile, Herbert's mother boarded a bus to Milton Park after she was chased by Samuel. She felt humiliated. First, her son, Lameck had told her off, and Samuel had literally thrown her out of his parents' house. When she got to her son's house, and especially when she saw Herbert's car parked in the driveway, she began to wail uncontrollably. But she was greeted with an unusual silence when she got to the house. Aida was not there. She called out but nobody answered. She went outside and asked the gardener where Herbert had gone. He told her that he had not seen Herbert leave the house, so he went and knocked on the door. There was no response.

Herbert woke up and went to the staff quarters looking for John, the gardener. That's when he saw his mother, who had gone to wait for him there. He looked tired and haggard. His eyes were red and puffy. He noticed that his mother's eyes were puffy, too, from crying. They went to the main house together, where they exchanged their ordeals

"Aida left me, *Amai.*" Herbert said shedding tears.

"It's all because of Netsai. She is the cause of this entire bad omen. If she doesn't want you anymore, why can't she just leave you in peace instead of bringing bad luck into your life? You are not the first man to practice polygamy. I don't see why people should fuss about it. I told her parents off."

"I didn't know you were going there?"

"Why couldn't I? You think giving birth is an easy thing? No person is going to mess with my son and expect me to keep quiet. I saw her stubborn brother, that one called Samuel and he accused me of witchcraft," *Va*Soda said.

"Did he...?"

"That's not all. He dragged me out of their house. I was treated like a dog, my son." She began to cry. Herbert was also crying. There was no one to comfort them.

CHAPTER seventeen

Netsai returned from Samuel's house after a month, and began to go about her everyday business as usual. She was walking to a Mother's Union church service at her church, when the women walking behind her began to talk about her.

"You know what, I forgot to tell you something," one woman known as *Amai*Rumbi, said to the rest of the women.

"Umm, what's the latest?" *Amai*Samson asked. She liked gossiping. Because they were walking very close to Netsai, *Amai*Rumbi used facial expressions to indicate that she was talking about Netsai.

"I will tell you more after the church service and meeting," she said.

They caught up with Netsai and greeted her as if they had not been gossiping about her a few seconds earlier.

"How are you, Mrs Kudzingwa?" *Amai*Samson greeted Netsai.

"I am well, if you are well," Netsai replied.

"We hardly see you at the women's meetings these days, or are you attending the Mothers' Union on Saturdays instead, Mrs Kudzingwa?" *Amai*Rumbi asked.

"I wasn't around, that's all."

Netsai made it obvious that she was in no mood for a chit-chat. She slowed her pace and the two women walked past her, Netsai knew that the two women were in the habit of pretending to like someone when in actual fact they would be digging for information to gossip about. She knew they laughed at what was going on in her life.

The two women arrived at the church a few minutes before it started. That gave them ample time to gossip, even in the house of the Lord.

"That woman is evil. She reported her husband to the police and had him arrested. Imagine, a Christian doing that," *Amai*Rumbi said.

"Maybe she listened to that rubbish said by the policemen who came to educate us about domestic violence and reporting abusive husbands to the police," *Amai*Samson suggested.

"That policeman was only doing his job. A woman, who goes to church, belongs to the Mothers' Union, and wears the church uniform, should not do anything like that."

"I heard that she was living in Borrowdale at her brother's place. That's why we were not seeing her at church meetings."

"A woman who sends her husband to jail must be named and shamed. I am going to preach about her deeds today. Shameless woman!" *Amai*Rumbi said.

When her time to preach came, she went to the pulpit where she read from the book of Ruth, about a daughter-in-law who followed her mother-in-law after the death of her husband.

"And yet there are some of us in this congregation who have thrown away the values of married life. They fail to honour their husbands when they are still alive. Would they follow their mothers-in-law when their husbands die, when they can not live with them when they are alive?"

"Hallelujah! Amen!" *Amai*Samson shouted.

"Marriage is not an institution to be taken for granted. It is a blessing from the Lord. We make pledges that until death do us part; yet we take the pleasure of reporting our husbands to the police when they reproach or beat us! What kind of a Christian woman does that?"

"Hallelujah, amen!" *Amai*Samson chorused.

"If Jesus, our Lord, could carry a cross which he was crucified on, why can't we carry the cross of marriage? A man is the head of the family. And a

Christian woman submits herself to her husband, and does not challenge his authority."

"Amen!"

"A woman who wears our blue or red uniform must live the way of Christians, not as a hypocrite who seeks Mammon and want to pursue Christian life at the same time. It's not easy to get to heaven if we don't mend our ways. What are title deeds? What is wrong for the father of your children to be the sole owner of the house you live in? Those are earthly riches. Remember when the Lord Jesus Christ was tested by the devil in the wilderness, he told the devil that man shall not live by bread alone, but by the word of God. Are title deeds not the same as the earthly riches the devil promised the Lord Jesus Christ if he worshipped him?"

"Amen, hallelujah!"

"The man is the head of the house. Women, if we are not careful, we might be worshipping the devil Lucifer instead of God. We should respect our husbands. If a husband takes another wife, ask yourself, where am I lacking? What is it that I am not doing, that I am supposed to be doing to force him to marry another wife, instead of packing bags and going to my parents' house? A happy man will never marry another wife. Correct your mistakes before you point fingers at others. If you are in this congregation and don't take heed of this, throw away your church uniform because heaven is very far away for you. We must teach our children to respect their fathers, and not to make fathers fear their children. Hell is coming, women. It is real! Run away from hell and seek heaven's gates. Women, don't bring shame on this congregation because people blame the church when they hear these things. Amen!" She concluded her sermon and broke into a song.

*"Kudenga hatisvike madzimai kana
tichida kupinda denga ngatizvipire,
Kudenga, Kudenga hakusi kwekutamba nako,*

> *Kudenga kudenga kunoenda vakasutswa*
> *naKiristo kwete naSatan."*

The other women joined in the song. Soon after the prayer, Netsai left the church and walked home. She knew that *Amai*Rumbi was preaching about her. When she arrived home, she took off the church uniform and threw it away. She was really angry.

The other women left the church meeting in small groups. Others were thanking *Amai*Rumbi for her well thought-out sermon, while others were asking who *Amai*Rumbi had been targeting in the sermon.

"Today's sermon was unusual. Who among us reported her husband to the police?" one woman asked.

"Ah, *Amai*Shupi, don't tell me that you didn't hear that Mrs Kudzingwa reported her husband to the police. She was talking about her," another woman volunteered the information.

"Shameless woman. How dare she preach about another person so directly? " Mrs Sibanda said. She was almost Netsai's age, and she was annoyed by *Amai*Rumbi's gospel. She didn't care if the other women heard her.

"You think she was referring to *Amai*Farai? Maybe it was just an ordinary sermon. You know, there are many times when you may think the sermon was about you, yet the preacher was only talking about everyday life," *Amai*Kuda suggested.

She knew that *Amai*Rumbi was targeting Netsai, but she wanted Mrs Sibanda to say more.

"She was talking about *Amai*Farai. Last week I heard her planning to shame her in church. " Mrs Sibanda said.

"But girls, let us be honest with each other, I will bury my uniform if being a Christian means that I can stand by and watch another woman enjoying the fruit of my sweat," Mrs Kunaka said.

"*Amai*Farai deserves our support instead of public humiliation. Next week if I am to take the pulpit I will preach in support of *Amai*Farai. We can not punish ourselves because of Christianity," other women laughed. "If *Amai*Rumbi has a personal vendetta against *Amai* Farai, she must resolve it outside the church walls instead of abusing the church platform to humiliate another woman."

Mrs Sibanda went to see Netsai, to strengthen her spirit and to tell her not to lose hope. She told her that other women in the church felt sorry for her, and supported her. Netsai felt better after the talk.

Herbert was now spending more time in Eastlea, after Aida had left. He was begging Netsai to remove her name on the house in Glen View, but Netsai would not have any of that. He gave various reasons for that, but Netsai refused to budge. Herbert was under pressure to return the money to the people who had paid him deposit for the house.

"Herbert, we have spoken about this issue before. I am not going to do anything like that, to remove my name from my house. Forget it," Netsai said, sipping her tea.

"You are an evil woman. You pretend to be a Christian when you are the devil," Herbert said.

"Herbert, if you think that I am a devil, fine! I am not bothered, you are entitled to your own opinion, but I am not budging as far as that house is concerned. I worked for it."

Herbert did not pursue the issue. He had been warned by the police that he would serve a long time in jail should he beat Netsai again.

"What else can I do, when my own wife has a team of lawyers, the police, and doctors to speak for her? You know what? I don't feel I am a man anymore. My household is now run by outside influences. My wife doesn't respect me anymore."

Netsai did not reply. Herbert put on his coat and bolted out of the house.

He decided to go and see Aida and his sons. Aida was now staying with her parents in Highfields high density township, because she wanted to 'fix' Herbert. She vowed to only come back to him if he put the house in her name, or at least buy her another house. Netsai had put a new tenant in the Milton Park house.

Each time Herbert went to Highfields to see Aida, he could not see her. She was avoiding him. Aida had rekindled her relationship with her previous boyfriend, a sugar daddy who was also very rich. When Herbert arrived at the house, he saw Aida getting out of her boyfriend's car at the gate. She pretended not to see Herbert.

"Aida! Aida!" Herbert called.

"What do you want from me, Herbert? Leave me alone," she said as she closed the gate behind her.

Herbert got out of the car and ran to the gate, and tried to touch Aida's shoulder. That enraged her.

"Don't touch me, Herbert!"

"Aida, I love you. You are my wife, please don't do this to me," he begged.

"Your wife? You must be out of your mind. What gives you the right to think that I am your wife? I don't associate with people who do not keep their promises, please never ever refer to me as your wife again. I am not your wife."

"But, Aida, I paid *lobola* for you. We have children together!"

"And you think paying *lobola* gives you a claim over me? How dare you think that? Idiot of man. Leave our gate, please."

Herbert could not believe what he was hearing. Aida had changed to become an aggressive lioness in the few months she had moved in with her parents.

"I am not your wife, so please, don't ever come here again." Aida walked away. He followed her and grabbed her hand.

"Please, can you let go of me, please!" Aida begged, but Herbert wouldn't let go.

There was a commotion, which brought Aida's sister-in-law, her brother's wife's running outside.

Herbert released Aida's hand, and the sister-in-law started retreating to the house but Aida called her back.

"*Amai*Aida, can you come back?" The sister-in-law, who had a child named after Aida, came back.

"I called you here to be my witness." Aida said, fishing Z$2 from her wallet. "Here, Herbert, this is my *gupuro*, divorce token. We were finished the day I walked out of your house. It's over. You can show your mother this token." She handed the money to Herbert, who took it in disbelief.

"Are you crazy, Aida? Where have you seen a woman giving a man *gupuro*?"

"You think *gupuro* is a one-way system? A woman can also divorce a man, Herbert, so please, can you go away?"

Herbert looked at Aida. "You are mad! You are my wife and the mother of my children I am not going to let you go," his voice was raised. He was angry.

"So what will you do to me? Don't even dare to beat me, because I will teach you a lesson. You can beat Netsai and not me."

"You have been given gupuro, a divorce token, so please stop making noise for us. You are now trespassing," *Amai*Aida said.

"You forget about my *lobola* you accepted? I will beat you up," Herbert said. "You used my money and now you ill-treat me," he was angry and ready to hit *Amai*Aida.

"Did I use your money? What are you talking about, you foolish man?" She was angry. When the *lobola* for Aida was paid she had been the one at the forefront, off-loading the parcels.

Within a few minutes, there was a crowd of people at the gate, people who had come to watch the free drama. Aida's relatives who were in the house came outside, including their lodgers. Herbert began to explain his story to one of Aida's aunts.

"*Tete*, can you see what your niece is doing to me. How can she give me Z$2 and say it's gupuro, a divorce token?" He showed Aida's aunt the money.

"If you are divorced, what do you want me to do? She doesn't love you anymore so please respect her wishes," Aida's aunt said.

Herbert could not believe his ears.

"*Tete*, how can you support this, after all that I have done for your family? I paid a lot of money for Aida, and now you do this to me?"

"Where you forced to fork out the money? Aida has another boyfriend who is ready to marry her. A man who will provide for her and not one who would use her like you did. You are a foolish man, a *fourteen*! You think you can match yourself to Aida? "

"Oh, you now call me a *fourteen*, a foolish man?" Herbert was angry.

"Are you not? We are finished with you, sir. We did not take money from your pockets. You gave it to us. Clever birds build their nests using other birds' feathers. That is what happened to you, so leave now," Aida's aunt was a rude woman. "Stupid man!" She kicked Herbert. She turned to her niece. "Aida, what had you seen in this idiot?"

A woman, a tenant at Aida's parents' house came to the scene holding a hoe. Herbert thought she was going to hit him with the hoe and covered his face in defence. Everyone laughed.

"You are a coward!" someone called from the crowd.

"Here, if you don't think that the Z$2 is enough for *gupuro*, we will do it the traditional way; when men used to give women hoes as divorce tokens. Herbert, this hoe is a divorce token given to you by Aida, go and begin a new life," the woman put the hoe near to Herbert.

Herbert could not stand the humiliation anymore. Someone in Aida's house began playing a song, *Anodyiwa haataure* by System Tazvida, which meant that when someone squandered their money in pleasure, they have themselves to blame. He knew the crowd could get ugly any time, so he took to his heels and fled.

"We will see each other in court when I come to claim maintenance for the children." Aida shouted after him. Herbert was too scared of the crowd to go to his car. He ran and walked, and ran again, still holding the Z$2 in his hand. Herbert had temporarily lost his sanity. He could not believe that Aida's family had treated him so badly. To think that he had depleted almost all his family's resources trying to support Aida and her family. He thought he saw a crowd of people following him and ran even faster, towards Bulawayo Road. He was also thinking of the people he owed money, and the humiliation by Aida's family, and wished for death to consume him.

Aida saw Herbert's car still parked outside. She thought Herbert would come back to collect it, but he was nowhere to be seen. She took the spare keys from her bag and drove the car to Netsai's house. She left it just outside the gate and threw the spare keys into the yard. She had asked her friend to follow her to Netsai's house because she wanted the friend to drive her back home. She did not want to get any bad omen from the car, should anything happen to Herbert. She returned to Highfields with her friend.

Netsai found the car keys and the car abandoned near her gate when she was escorting her sister-in-law who had visited her. Netsai had been telling Samuel's wife about her desire to get a divorce and move on when she found Herbert's car abandoned at the gate. At first she thought that Herbert had come home drunk and dropped the keys, but he was nowhere to be seen.

Herbert walked along Bulawayo road, talking to himself. He was also crying. When he got tired, he sat down by the roadside with his jacket in his hand. A car pulled up near him to drop off a passenger. It was a commuter bus headed for Bulawayo. The driver asked Herbert if he was waiting for a lift to Bulawayo, but he received no response from Herbert. The driver saw that Herbert was crying, so he got out of the car and walked towards him, all the while asking what the matter was.

"He looks like he has just been robbed," one woman who was a passenger in the car said. "This is a very dangerous spot. Thieves and robbers like waylaying people here," she continued.

Herbert did not say anything. He sobbed even more. He showed the driver the Z$2.

"They gave me this Z$2." The driver thought the thieves who had robbed him only left him the Z$2 for transport.

"You can come with us, sir. We can take you to Bulawayo if that is where you are going. We will not make you pay," the driver said, feeling sorry for Herbert. He stood up and got into the car.

"These thieves are shameless and heartless. How can they leave someone with only Z$2?" someone in the car said.

"What if he is a thief?" one man suggested. Thieves could do anything to get attention so as to rob their victims while they are unaware.

"I am not a thief. I am a victim of...." Herbert said, but did not finish what he wanted to say because he was overcome by tears. The men helped him get into the car and off to Bulawayo they went.

"I think the thieves hit him. I noticed that he was limping," the woman said. She did not know that Herbert had tripped and fallen as he ran away from Aida's place. But the woman had the surprise of her life when Herbert, who had been dozing on the seat, began shouting that all women were crazy, one had stolen his house while another had given him $2. The man sitting next to him nudged him in the rib in an effort to wake him up.

"These women are cruel, brother Lameck. They stole everything from me...!" He woke up.

"Women of today? They also train in kick-boxing and karate," a man, who was also a passenger in the car commented. He thought Herbert had been robbed by women along the Bulawayo Road where they had found him.

"Women are even more dangerous than men. They can do anything. I don't trust women anymore," another man said.

"Even robbing people? It's hard to believe," another one said.

Herbert couldn't agree more. He just nodded his head.

"They took everything from me," Herbert said.

"You should be grateful that they did not kill you. At least you are alive," the first woman said. "It could have been worse."

They talked about women and the evil things women were now doing till they reached Bulawayo, but Herbert did not participate since he had gone back to sleep. The driver left Herbert at the main bus station called Renkin. He also gave him Z$20.

Herbert got out of the car and began to walk around Bulawayo. That's when it hit him that he was very far from his home and family. He was in Bulawayo where he could hardly understand the language.

* * *

Meanwhile, Netsai and other relatives were looking for Herbert. The following day he did not report for work, and that's when Netsai decided to go to the police and file a missing person's report. They searched everywhere even in the rivers, suspecting that he had committed suicide. The police thought Herbert had either committed suicide because he did not want to pay back the deposit he had collected from the people when he was trying to sell the Glen View house, or that he had feigned disappearance, yet he was well and living somewhere else. Aida was bothered by the police for a long time, because she had been the one last person to have seen Herbert. The police opened a docket for the disappearance of Herbert. It was only after four months that Netsai received a letter from Herbert. The letter was stamped in Bulawayo, but was written on a very dirty piece of paper and posted with insufficient postage. There was no returning address.

Dear AmaiFarai,

How are you and the children? I am fine. Don't look for me, I am alive and well.

Yours truly,
BabavaFarai.

Netsai took the letter to Herbert's brother, Lameck, and showed it to him. They took the letter to the police, who asked Lameck to verify if that was indeed Herbert's handwriting. Lameck agreed that to his best knowledge, it was his brother's handwriting. The police sent his photographs to Bulawayo police to see if they could find him there, but nothing positive came from Bulawayo. After five years, the police closed both the docket and missing person's file. There was speculation that he could have crossed the border into South Africa or Botswana. None of them could have imagined it, but Herbert was now roaming the streets of Bulawayo as a heavy drunkard and a gambler. Returning to Harare was not an option for him because he was in debt.

CHAPTER Eighteen

It wasn't easy for Netsai to pull her resources together and start a new life. But with Herbert missing and out of her life, she was able to collect money for rent from the other houses and repay the mortgages, which were now in arrears. The people who had paid some money to Herbert lost their case in the court. The courts ruled in Netsai's favour because during the time they paid Herbert the money for deposit, they had not checked to see the title deeds of the house to establish if it was only Herbert Kudzingwa registered on the house or not. The people had argued that they had known Herbert from when he was building the house, so they had no reason to doubt that he was the only owner of the house. However, because by the time they had entered into an agreement of sale with Herbert, Netsai had already applied for an injunction through the courts to stop Herbert from selling the house, they lost the case.

Eventually she managed to revive her sewing business and it was easy for her to get her customers back, because customers in the hairdressing and sewing industry tend to be loyal to their suppliers or hairdressers. She took a loan from the bank and opened a small factory, making cement bricks and blocks for dura walls. Many people were building houses in newly serviced middle-density suburbs of Glen View, Warren Park and other parts of Harare. To Netsai that was a good business venture, and she ended up successful and employed many people.

She also opened a nursery for children, which was also a well paying business. She had returned to the Netsai of the old days.

She decided to celebrate the fifth anniversary of her building factory by throwing a huge party for her workers. Someone at the gate pressed the intercom, while they were in the middle of celebrating. Tsitsi asked who it was, but after getting no response, she decided to go and check. She went with Rutendo, who was now more than eight years old.

"Hello Tsitsi," the man looking like a tramp said. "How are you Tsitsi?" She realized that it was Herbert.

"I am well, if you are well *Baba*," Tsitsi replied.

"Who is that, *sisi* Tsitsi?" Rutendo asked.

"It's your dad," she replied.

"You are kidding! My dad? How come he looks different from the one on the pictures?" Rutendo said, as she reached out to Herbert. She shook his hand, and felt his rough hands closing on her tiny soft palms. "You can come inside, daddy. We are having a party," Rutendo said as she dragged her father through the gate.

Tsitsi did not know what to do. She wanted to leave Herbert outside the gate and ask Netsai to go and deal with him, but after seeing how happy Rutendo was, she let him through.

Netsai got the shock of her life when she saw Herbert coming towards the house. He looked like a tramp. His hair was greyish and unkempt; his shoes looked two sizes bigger because he was dragging his feet. They were tied with shoelaces of different colours. His jacket looked as if it was hanging on a tree. The trousers looked very short; torn too, above the ankles.

Farai and Samuel looked through the window and saw Herbert. As they walked towards the gate, the intercom buzzed again. They went to check. It was Herbert's mother, *Va*Soda. Farai stared at his father. He did not know whether to hug him or ignore him. Samuel looked at *Va*Soda and hissed through his teeth, loud enough for her to hear. Netsai also came out of the house, and with arms akimbo, watched the drama. Netsai's sister, Tanya came out of the house, too. She was drunk.

"Excuse me, dear Lord God, am I seeing really well or I am going mad?" She shouted. Netsai's parents, who had followed their daughter outside, now stood behind Netsai and Samuel.

"Hello, B*abava*Farai," Netsai extended her hand to Herbert after a while. Herbert nervously took her hand as if afraid that he would be beaten.

"I saw your husband come to the village and he said he wanted to see his family. I decided to come with him. I met someone I know near your gate, that is why I did not come in at the same time with B*abava*Farai," *Va*Soda explained.

She was lying. The truth was that she had stopped near the gate to administer the magic concoction she had been given by a traditional healer to make Netsai's heart melt once she saw Herbert. During the week Herbert had been at the village, they had visited all kinds of traditional healers in order to get different types of potions.

"How are you, *Amai*?" Netsai asked, extending her hand to *Va*Soda.

"I am well, if you are well my beloved *muroora*."

Netsai's parents greeted *Va*Soda. Samuel was angry. He refused to shake her hand, or acknowledge Herbert. Herbert was embarrassed and was wishing for the earth to open up and swallow him. Farai went to stand near his mother as if to protect her. Tariro, who was watching the whole scene through the window, did not bother to go and greet her father. Tanya broke into a popular song by Susan Mapfumo, called "*Kwenya Mhezi Dzako wega Makeyi*", meaning scratch yourself my friend or sort out your problems my friend.

Rutendo dragged her father towards the house, Herbert looked at Netsai as if to ask for permission, but Netsai was expressionless. Her response was difficult to read.

"*Muroora*, I know that your husband wronged you, but can you find a place in your heart to forgive him? He is the father of your children." *Va*Soda begged, clapping her hands. Netsai did not reply.

"To forgive this bastard, are you mad?" Samuel interjected.

"Leave Aunt Netsai to make her decision, *Babava*Ruvimbo," his wife pleaded.

"Netsai my daughter, take your husband back. Wealth is meaningless if you don't have a partner to share it with. I know you have cars, houses, and businesses, but your life is empty without a husband...." Netsai's mother begged. She was, however, interrupted by a phone call for Netsai. Tariro said it was from the builders working on their house in Westgate, where Netsai was building a new house.

"Tell them I am in a meeting and I will call them when I am finished. Tell them the meeting will take a little long," Netsai instructed Tariro.

Netsai took her wallet, which was in her pocket. She opened the wallet slowly as if gauging the mood of the people. She fished a crisp Z$100 note.

"Don't divorce me, *Amaiva*Farai, please. Don't give me another gupuro, divorce token." Herbert began to walk towards the gate because he did not want to be humiliated again in front of all the people. But when he got to the gate, he saw his brother Lameck and his family parking their car. They were also coming for the party. Lameck nearly choked with shame and rage when he saw Herbert. Herbert was behaving like a mad man. Lameck took his brother and put him in the car. He went into the yard and saw his mother. He took her to the car as well and drove them away, to his house. He was really embarrassed by the whole situation. Netsai looked at the car until it had disappeared. She closed the gate.

THE END

OTHER BOOKS BY THE SAME AUTHOR

1. Zimbabwe Township Music

Zimbabwe Township Music Book is a celebration of age-old popular music, which was evolved by the early urban settlers as far back as the 1930's. Urban Culture in those days was a product of mixed traditional, contemporary and Western influences, which all moulded into the unique township music. It is therefore the musical offspring and melodic fusion of several tribal and cultural urban settlers in the early Black townships; typified by such variance as kwela, tsabatsaba, marabi and afro-jazz.

Township Music often became a symbol of identity and dissent in Black townships, which did not go so well with the authorities of the day. As the political situation became tense, the music went under around 1963, when the Federation of Rhodesia and Nyasaland came to an end. At Zimbabwe's independence in 1980, Township Music resurfaced and trickled slowly back into the country, to a much awaited reception and revival.

Today the Township Music craze is gripping the country, drawing even youthful enthusiasts in its wake. It has continued to grow and is taking the country by storm. The book features artist like Dorothy Masuka, August Musarurwa, Sonny Sondo, Simangaliso Tutani, Jacob Mhungu, John White, Prudence Katomeni Mbofana, Tanga wekwa Sando and Louis Mhlanga, the music appears to have caught the world, too, in its grip.

2. **USENZENI**

Set in the late 1980s, the book takes the reader into the life of Senzeni, the main character in the book. Capturing the 'situation on the ground' An African mother who vows to reach the ends of the earth to better her child beyond what she herself has been; she typically fights this battle without the support of her husband who invariably drinks his money away and yet expects the world to keep running efficiently around him.

The ending of the story shows just how immaculately fertile a burnt field becomes, especially when good rains fall on it, because Senzeni's terrible situation leads not only to her rise as an independent success but also to the success of her mother and grandmother.

Three generations are empowered in the process of saving Senzeni because the women closest to Senzeni who have for all their lives been dominated and subordinated by males come to determine their own fate in such an exemplary way which leads all men to sit back and really consider how much they have hindered or held back the women in their lives.

3. WOMEN MUSICIANS OF ZIMBABWE 1930's TO 2013

Women Musicians of Zimbabwe Book is a celebration of Women's Struggle for Voice and Artistic Expression. The book explains how Zimbabwean women musicians have claimed their place in the music industry since the 1930s.

Despite the Zimbabwean deeply rooted patriarchal system, women have played an important role in the evolution of popular music nevertheless.
The contribution of women to the evolution of musical styles from the pre-colonial times to the present is outlined.
- Township Music/Jazz, the American, South African, Zimbabwean Mix 1930's-1950's
- Mbaqanga, Rhumba, Reggae and Soul 1960's-1970's
- Traditional/Popular music mostly from 1970's to 2000
- Urban Grooves Music: Zimbabwean Rap/Hip Hop/House/Disco – 2001
- Church Music/Gospel Music 2000-

Some of the women who feature prominently are: Dorothy Masuka, Susan Chenjerayi, Virginia Sillah, Susan Mapfumo, Stella Chiweshe, Irene Chigamba, Shuvai Wutaunashe, Prudence Katomeni Mbofana and Chiwoniso Maraire.

THE AUTHOR

Joyce Jenje Makwenda was born in 1958 in Mbare Township in Harare. She is a researcher, writer and producer. For the past 30 years or more, she has been involved in research in the areas of music, popular culture, media, politics, women's histories and gender issues. Joyce has made some notable achievements with her artistic work across the board, winning a number of awards since the early 1990's.

Printed in the United States
By Bookmasters